The case had only one drawback…

The sizzling attraction that had hit him the first moment he'd laid eyes on Alonsa. The way she'd moved, the way she'd felt in his arms when they'd two-stepped their way through the sultry country-western ballad. The way she looked now in the chair with her legs curled up under her.

Everything about her turned him on.

But seducing her was not in the rules of engagement. It would make him less effective in finding her daughter, would complicate things until working together would be impossible. Worse, it would be taking advantage of her at her weakest and most vulnerable.

He'd just have to keep his libido under control…at least until he found out what happened to her little girl. That would require seeing Alonsa without touching her and going home to cold showers and an empty bed.

And he thought the _____ ugh.

BRAVO, TANGO, COWBOY

BY
JOANNA WAYNE

First published in Great Britain 2010
Harlequin Mills & Boon Limited,
Eton House, 18-24 Paradise Road, Richmond, Surrey TW9 1SR

© Jo Ann Vest 2009

ISBN: 978 0 263 88281 0

46-1210

Harlequin Mills & Boon policy is to use papers that are natural, renewable
and recyclable products and made from wood grown in sustainable forests.
The logging and manufacturing processes conform to the legal environmental
regulations of the country of origin.

Printed and bound in Spain
by Litografia Rosés S.A., Barcelona

Joanna Wayne was born and raised in Shreveport, Louisiana, and received her undergraduate and graduate degrees from LSU-Shreveport. She moved to New Orleans in 1984, and it was there that she attended her first writing class and joined her first professional writing organization. Her first novel, *Deep in the Bayou*, was published in 1994. Now, dozens of published books later, Joanna has made a name for herself on the cutting edge of romantic suspense in both series and single-title novels. She has been on the Waldenbooks bestsellers list for romance and has won many industry awards. She is a popular speaker at writing organizations and local community functions, and has taught creative writing at the University of New Orleans Metropolitan College. She currently resides in a small community forty miles north of Houston, Texas, with her husband. Though she still has many family and emotional ties to Louisiana, she loves living in the Lone Star state. You may write Joanna at PO Box 265, Montgomery, Texas 77356, USA.

To mothers everywhere who know
what it means to love a child with all your heart.

Chapter One

The moonlit night was made for romance. Alonsa Salatoya stood alone, fighting the salty tears that wet her dark eyes and threatened to make a black sea of her mascara as the newlyweds two-stepped across the portable dance floor. Love was a beautiful thing—while it lasted.

The night's hostess, Linney Martin, stepped to her side. "Dani and Marcus make a beautiful couple, don't they?"

Alonsa nodded. "They do, and they seem totally in love."

"Yep. They were meant for each other."

"Something tells me your infamous matchmaking skills had a hand in getting them together."

"Not this time. Their relationship sprang from a chance meeting at the Renaissance Festival. Didn't I tell you that story?"

"Only part of it." Alonsa had met the bride and groom on a couple of occasions but didn't really qualify as a friend. Yet Linney had practically insisted she attend the affair to celebrate their recent wedding.

Perhaps because there were so few magnificent parties such as this in the small, rural town of Dobbin, Texas.

"Their story is fascinating," Linney said. "I'll fill you in when we go shopping in Conroe for the fabric to re-cover those chairs in the guest suite. But speaking of matchmaking, there's probably one or two nice cowboys here tonight I could introduce you to."

That explained the invitation. "I came with a guy," Alonsa reminded her. "A very charming man."

"Your boss, who just happens to be gay," Linney said.

"Gay and a magnificent dancer," Alonsa countered. "In my book that makes him the perfect escort."

If you wanted to be exact, she wasn't his guest tonight. Always the businessman, Esteban had invited a new customer named Keidra Shelton in that capacity. Keidra had recently moved to the Woodlands and wanted an extreme makeover for the interior of her house, a cosmopolitan look that captured the spirit of her new state. Esteban had decided Alonsa was the perfect person to create that.

He and Keidra had picked up Alonsa and driven her to the party. The woman had talked too much and asked far too many questions about Alonsa's personal life and how she'd come to live in a small, rural town like Dobbin. Other than that, she was nice enough and Alonsa looked forward to the challenge of creating an interior that worked for her.

Linney tossed her head, tinkling the diamond earrings that dangled from her earlobes. "Matchmaking and taking advantage of a good situation is one thing, but those women are taking it a tad too far." She nodded toward the bar that had been set up in a corner of the sprawling white tent.

Alonsa instantly spotted the women who'd fueled Linney's ire. The object of their lustful attentions was a man in a black tux and cowboy boots. His dark, thick hair had an unruly bent as he leaned his hard, lean body closer to the attractive redhead who was officially Esteban's guest for the evening.

Alonsa didn't recognize the other two ladies, but one couldn't have been more than eighteen and the other had to be pushing sixty. Keidra was probably in her early thirties. The man had all the bases covered.

"Romeo must be new in town. I haven't seen him around before."

"Brand-new. Hawk is Cutter's latest recruit for the Double M Investigation and Protection Service. He's living in the cabin on the ranch that Marcus recently vacated."

"Hawk? Is that a nickname or a description?"

Linney laughed. "A bit of both. He was a civilian helicopter pilot before he joined the service and became a SEAL."

"So he's another of Cutter's Special Ops recruits?"

"Yes. Infamous, or so I hear. He was awarded several medals. Cutter and Marcus both swear he can not only walk on water but he can take down an enemy a half mile away while he's doing it."

"Yet he looks every inch the dashing cowboy."

"There is that. Him I suggest you avoid unless you're strictly out for a good time."

Which was exactly what Linney had told her only days ago that she needed.

As if on cue, Hawk turned and spotted them staring at him. He smiled and tipped his glass in their direction. Alonsa's eyes met his and her insides reacted with a surprising quiver. She looked away so fast she grew dizzy.

It was the champagne, she decided. This was only her second glass but it would be her last drink of the evening. Good time or not, a womanizer in Western boots was the last thing she needed.

"I'm really glad you came tonight," Linney said, bringing Alonsa back into the moment. "You need to get out more."

"So you've told me before, but it's not like I'm a hermit," Alonsa protested.

"I know. You go to work, but other than that, you pretty much stay cooped up inside that ranch house."

"A *huge* ranch house, and I have a three-year-old son to keep me busy. But you're right. I should get out more. Thanks for inviting me."

"So here you are. I've been looking all over for you," Cutter said, joining them and slipping an arm around Linney.

"Alonsa and I were just watching your friend Hawk in action," Linney said. "He's already collected a harem of admirers and this is only his second week in town."

"As long as you're not one of them," Cutter said, leaning over to kiss his wife on the back of the neck.

"Not a chance. I've got my cowboy."

"Good. Hold that thought. Not that I'm not grateful to have Hawk join up with me."

"Do you need a pilot?" Alonsa asked.

"I need another good man. Hawk Taylor's the best

and the reason I, and more than a few others, are back on U.S. soil and breathing instead of being feasted on by worms on the other side of the world."

Linney slipped her arm around her husband's waist. "You never told me Hawk saved your life."

"You never asked. Now, if I'm not mistaken, the band is playing our song. Will you excuse us, Alonsa, while I dance with my gorgeous wife?"

"Absolutely."

Alonsa watched the two of them walk away, so in love that they glowed brighter than the tiny white lights that twinkled above them. For now, they had it all. Alonsa had been there once. It seemed eons ago.

IT WAS A HELL OF A post-wedding celebration. A great band, free-flowing alcohol, beautiful women and all out in the wide-open spaces of the Double M Ranch. But the best part of it all was that Hawk was not the sucker who'd just bought in to the fantasy of marital bliss.

Been there, done that, had the scars and the holes in his bank account to prove it. Give him a reconnaissance mission over a heavily armed enemy anytime. At least then you knew they'd be gunning for you. Not that the divorce hadn't been mainly his fault. He'd only been half there and only half the time. The only people he'd ever truly committed to was his team of rowdy frogmen.

"Care to dance?"

The woman asking and looking up at him with a pair of gorgeous blue eyes was a hottie who'd been semi-stalking him all night. He'd met her at the champagne fountain earlier. She was a secretary to one of the local congressmen—or was she his daughter? Anyway there was a correlation.

The band broke into a new number, but this time instead of a nice boot-scooting beat, the tune had a Latin rhythm. "I'd love to dance with you, but I'm afraid that's not in my repertoire," he said. "But look me up for a two-step, and I'm all yours."

"Promise?"

"On a stack of James Bond novels."

Another guy came along and tugged her onto the floor with a few other brave couples. They weren't bad. One couple were obvious graduates of a course in ballroom dancing, probably recently. The man's mouth moved as he counted the tango beats. The woman was as stiff as MRE rations.

A debonair, slightly past middle-age man with thinning salt-and-pepper hair stepped onto the dance floor. Accompanying him was the gorgeous dark-haired woman Hawk had spotted earlier standing with Linney.

The sapphire-blue dress she was wearing curved about her like silken skin, not so tight she looked trampy, but fitted enough that there was no denying she had a dynamite body. A tempting amount of cleavage showed. Not nearly enough, in Hawk's opinion.

The hemline cleared her thighs, but there was plenty of bare leg left to appreciate. Great calves, superb ankles and a pair of silver stiletto heels that did their best to show off the sexy features.

None of that compared to how she looked when she started to dance. Hawk had been near explosions that weren't half as hot.

Linney stepped up beside him and linked her arm

with his. "Need a napkin to wipe that drool from your lips, cowboy?"

"I might. Who's the temptress?"

"My interior decorator."

"Yeah, well, I'm feeling in need of a major overhaul. Is that her husband she's dancing with?"

"No. She's a widow with a young son."

She looked as if she were about to say more, but didn't.

"So is the dude she's dancing with her lover?"

"He's her boss. Esteban of Esteban's Western Interiors."

"And does the temptress have a name?"

"Alonsa Salatoya, but she's had a really rough life the last few years, Hawk. I don't want to see her hurt again, so let's just say she's off-limits to you."

"You don't really believe all those wild heartbreaker tales Cutter and Marcus spread about me, do you?"

"Shouldn't I?"

"Strictly jealousy on their part," he teased.

"What about the women swooning in your wake all night?"

"It's the boots. Women love 'em."

"Every guy in Texas has boots."

"Must be my cologne, then."

"Collect all the hearts you want, Hawk. Just not Alonsa's. Not that I actually think you could. As far as I know she hasn't had a date since her husband died."

"So she's a recent widow?"

"It's been two years."

The music stopped and Esteban dipped his partner so low that the two were practically parallel to the floor. Her hem inched upward. Hawk felt a tightening in his groin. Staying clear of Alonsa was probably a warning he should heed, but not for the reasons Linney had stated. He just wasn't up to dealing with the emotional entanglements of dating a woman who'd been grieving for two years, especially a woman with a kid.

When the dancing duo righted themselves, they headed for the edge of the dance floor. Linney waved them over. "You two were magnificent," she raved. "It was like having a filming of *Dancing with the Stars* right here at the Double M."

"Alonsa makes any man look good on the dance floor," Esteban said.

She gave a mock bow. "A woman is only as good as her partner."

That might be true about some things, but Hawk figured Alonsa would look good dancing with a battery-operated frog. Her gaze met Hawk's for the briefest of seconds and he was mesmerized by their dark mystic depths.

The band hit up a version of "Crazy."

"I love this song," Linney said, looking up at Esteban as she started to sway.

"Would you care to dance?" he asked.

"I'd love to."

They disappeared onto the dance floor, leaving Hawk alone with Alonsa.

"I think we've been set up," Alonsa said.

That wouldn't get any complaints from him, but... "Actually, I was warned by Linney to stay clear of you."

"I got the same warning. I suspect it was to make certain we noticed each other."

"Ah, the old reverse psychology."

"Afraid so. Linney's been back in Dobbin less than a year but already her matchmaking schemes are infamous. I guess it's understandable, though. She's so happy with Cutter that she wants that for everyone."

"Then I guess we should at least dance," Hawk said. "We don't want to disappoint our hostess."

"I'm afraid she's doomed to disappointment with me."

"Why is that?"

"Nothing personal, but I've adjusted quite well to not having a man in my life."

"I asked for a dance, not matching towels."

She reddened a little. "In that case, I accept the offer."

"Don't expect any fancy footwork," he cautioned. "Unlike your previous partner, I'm your basic shuffle and snuggle kind of dancer."

"Just don't stamp on my toes. These shoes are painful enough as it is."

"And worth every throb." He took her hand and led her onto the floor. Her fragrance was intoxicating, kind of like a sunny summer morning after a hard rain. He pulled her into his arms. He was tall enough that even in her nosebleed heels, she fit in his arms just right, cheek to cheek, hip to hip, thigh to thigh. Arousal coiled around his insides like a corkscrew.

She put her mouth to his ear and he felt the heat of her breath on his neck. "You are a much better dancer than you admitted," she crooned.

"Like your boss said, you'd make any man look good."

"I had a lot of practice," she admitted. "I took lessons for most of my life and danced on Broadway for years."

"From Broadway to Dobbin, Texas. That's some detour."

"It happens."

She didn't offer more and Hawk didn't push. He didn't intend to be manipulated into a relationship by Linney, but that didn't mean he couldn't enjoy having a beautiful, sensual woman in his arms.

Alonsa's small, satin bag was buzzing against the table when they returned. She reached inside and grabbed her vibrating cell phone. He heard just enough to know that the call concerned her son.

"I have to find Esteban," she said as soon as she broke the connection.

"What's wrong?"

"That was my babysitter. My son fell and hit his head. She doesn't think it's serious, but it's bleeding and he's crying. He's only three. I need to check on him."

"No need to find Esteban. I can drive you if it's a ride you're looking for."

"That's not necessary."

"It could be. Esteban's car may be blocked in. My truck isn't." He'd made sure of that just in case he decided to sneak out early. He didn't usually last more than an hour or so at fancy shindigs like this one.

Alonsa scanned the parking area. "Surely the parking valet could get Esteban's car out."

"You'd save time if I drive you, but hey, it's your kid. Your call."

That seemed to resonate with her. "If you're sure you don't mind?"

"Wouldn't have offered if I did."

"Then I just need to let Esteban know so he won't look for me later."

"There's Cutter," Hawk said, nodding toward his

former SEAL buddy and new boss, who was standing nearby talking to a couple of local ranchers. "We'll tell him. He'll see that Esteban gets the word."

She nodded and in minutes they were on their way to her place. It hit Hawk about five miles down the road that with the help of a bleeding kid, he had played exactly into Linney's matchmaking scheme.

BRANDON SALATOYA'S injury turned out to be no more than a bump on the head and a slight cut across the top of his right eye. The rambunctious preschooler had reportedly been running up the stairs for his bedtime story when he'd tripped over his dog, a short-tailed, mixed-breed mutt with soulful eyes and a yappy bark.

The boy had settled down quickly when his mother arrived and was now drinking chocolate milk and marching a plastic dinosaur over a mountain of sofa cushions. He'd gotten a reprieve from bedtime until Alonsa was certain there was no aftereffect from the bump to the head.

The sitter, a rawboned rancher's wife named Ellen, who smiled often and had graying, slightly frizzed hair, had gone home, greatly relieved that she hadn't allowed a serious injury on her watch.

Alonsa had disappeared with the promise to be right back. The dog, Carne, short for Carnivorous as the precocious youngster had explained, was lying by the fire in the massive stone fireplace, carefully keeping at least one eye on Hawk.

Had Linney been able to spy on them, she'd no doubt be pleased at the cozy, familial scene. But looks were deceiving. The coziness went no further than the visual effects. Once Alonsa was reassured her son was fine, having Hawk around had seemed to become instantly awkward for her.

He'd half expected her to push him out the door with the babysitter. Instead she'd offered to make a pot of coffee in a tone and manner that suggested she hoped he'd turn her down.

He hadn't, of course. Nothing intrigued him more than a woman not into him, especially one as provocative as Alonsa. When she walked, he envisioned her dancing on a Broadway stage, her body twisting and swaying into erotic choreographic movements.

Yet she was here in small-town Dobbin, Texas, living on a ranch with her young son, decorating other people's houses and playing ice princess to available suitors. He wondered what her husband had been like and how he'd died. And if his death was the explanation for the haunting shadows that lurked in the depths of Alonsa's dark eyes.

Brandon marched his dinosaur as close as he could to Hawk's leg without actually touching it. "How come you came to my house?"

"I gave your mother a ride home from the party."

"How come you're still here?"

Good question. "I'm going to have a cup of coffee with your mother."

"Why?"

"Because she asked me to."

"Why?"

Fortunately Alonsa picked that minute to rejoin them. "Don't go there with him," she cautioned Hawk. "The whys are a black hole from which there is no escape."

Hawk stood and took the cup of coffee she offered.

"I added a touch of Kahlúa and a dollop of whipped cream. If you'd rather have it plain, I can toss this and get you another cup."

He tasted the brew. "No, this is great."

"I'm sorry I rushed you away from the party. It's not that I don't trust Ellen. I do. She's raised five children of her own. It's just that I worry."

"No reason to apologize. Once you've toasted the newlyweds, the party's all downhill."

"You didn't look as if you were suffering," she teased.

"I've learned to hide it well." A comeback that wasn't that far from the truth.

Alonsa was still wearing the blue dress, but she'd slipped out of the metallic stiletto sandals and into a pair of cream-colored slippers. She'd also removed her necklace. The earrings still dangled seductively from her smooth lobes. Her lipstick had almost worn off completely, leaving her lips a glistening, pale pink.

She chose a seat across from him and Brandon, kicked off her slippers and curled her legs under her. "So what do you think of my designs?"

Design was probably the one thing of hers he hadn't been thinking about, especially since he had no clue what she was talking about. "Love them," he said, going for low-key enthusiasm.

"I first became interested in interior decorating while remodeling this house," she said. "I didn't get any formal training until after I'd moved to Dobbin."

"The house looks great." Actually it looked like he'd expect a ranch house to look, except…homier. Yep, that was the word he was looking for. The kind of house where a man could get comfortable with a good book—or a hot woman.

"I was going for rustic, but high-tech with modern comforts," she explained.

He gave the room a quick once-over. The walls were painted to look as if they were old stucco, with dents and nicks, in shades of a deep cream and pale tan. The chandelier looked as if it had once been used with gas. The mantel over the fireplace was thick, rough-hewn cypress, as were the high beams in the ceiling.

The wide wooden planks of the floor looked to be original to the house, but they were polished and partially covered by a woven rug that picked up the brown in the leather sofa. Two cane-covered rockers sat next to the fireplace.

"Looks like an authentic ranch house to me," he said. "And the sofa is definitely comfortable."

"Thanks. When my husband inherited the place, it was literally crumbling. We practically had to gut it."

"Then this is new construction?"

"All but the shell."

"Then you are good." The question was why would she go to all this trouble to live in Dobbin? "Do you have family in the area?"

"No."

"So how did you wind up here?"

Wrong question. He sensed as much as saw the instant change in her. She shuddered and wrapped her arms around herself, as if the room had suddenly dropped ten degrees, and then lowered her eyes to stare into her cup.

"My husband's uncle left him the ranch," she finally said. "Todd loved the place and always planned to retire here."

No mention as to how she felt about the house, yet her husband was dead and she'd stayed on. Must have been crazy about the man. Probably had him on a pedestal too high for any other man to ever climb.

"Do you want to see what I've done with the rest of the house?"

"Sure, as long as there won't be a test of my knowledge of the subject matter when we finish."

"No, but I can't promise not to bore you with details."

"You do and I'll start reciting the military handbook."

"Warning taken. Do you want to show Mr. Taylor your room, Brandon?"

The kid scrunched his nose and planted his dinosaur on top of his head, tangling the toy in the dark locks of hair. "No. Want to watch cartoons."

"Okay, but when I say it's bedtime, you have to turn off the TV without making a fuss."

He grinned as he hopped off the sofa and ran to retrieve a DVD from a basket on the bottom section of the built-in shelves. He inserted it into a player set between two stacks of children's books.

Hawk had yet to spot a TV. Alonsa picked up a remote, clicked it and then waited while the oil painting over the pine bookshelves slid away to reveal a flat-screen monitor.

"Impressive."

She smiled. It lit her face and softened all her

features. "Actually, the hidden TV is a bit of overkill, but it impresses potential clients."

"Then you work out of your home?"

"As much as I can. I don't like to spend any more time away from Brandon than I have to."

She went to the front door and checked the dead bolt, though he'd seen her lock it when she came in. "This way," she said, pausing to look out the window before she led him into the hallway.

Carne followed them. The intuitive dog definitely didn't trust Hawk with his mistress. Smart dog.

The kitchen was obviously Alonsa's masterpiece. She reveled in the explanation of how she'd sought to create a totally modern working arena without losing any of the ranch-house charm.

She'd done a bang-up job, right down to the red-and-white gingham curtains at the window and the appliances that were disguised as knotty pine cabinets. The awkwardness between them dropped away in layers as her enthusiasm built.

The kitchen phone rang. She grabbed the antique receiver. "It's probably Linney or Esteban making sure Brandon is okay." She put the receiver to her ear. Her hello was tentative.

A heartbeat later, her face turned a pasty white and her fingers trembled so badly the phone slipped from them. She swayed. Hawk caught her and the phone before either of them hit the floor.

She shook off the shock and grabbed the phone from him. "Lucy? Lucy, is that you?" Her voice bordered on hysteria.

Hawk shifted so that his ear was close enough for

him to hear a reply—had there been one. There was only the clanging of a receiver and the droll signal of a disconnected call.

Tears filled Alonsa's eyes.

His reaction system went on full alert. "Who was that?"

She looked away, avoiding eye contact. "No one."

"Like hell."

"It's nothing really."

"You're a wreck. If you tell me what's going on, I might be able to help."

"No one can help. Please, just go home, Hawk. Just go."

"Who's Lucy?"

"This isn't your concern." Her voice dropped to a shaky whisper.

Right. And he didn't need a strange woman's problems. So why wasn't he rushing out the door?

He took both her hands in his and waited until her gaze locked with his. "Who's Lucy?"

"My daughter. She was abducted two years ago."

Chapter Two

Alonsa pulled away from Hawk and walked to the kitchen window, staring out into the darkness but seeing nothing. She felt as if someone were scraping away the lining of her heart. The phone calls always had that effect on her.

The sound of breathing behind her was the only sign that Hawk was still in the room. She gathered her resolve slowly, giving her mind a chance to crawl out of the black abyss into which the call had sucked her. When she turned around, Hawk was only a few steps away, staring at her with concern etched into the lines of his face.

He leaned against the counter. "What's with the phone call?"

"A cruel hoax. It sounds like Lucy's voice, but it's not her."

His brows arched. "You sound sure of that."

"If it is her, it's a recording made right after she was abducted. She sounds exactly the same every time."

"How often do you get these calls?"

"It varies. In the beginning they came every week or

two. Then they slowed down to every few months, but they've picked up again over the last two months."

"Do you have a tracer on your phone?"

"Yes, but it doesn't help. The calls last only a few seconds and the ones they have been able to trace only match prepaid cell phones from locations all the way from Florida to California."

"Strange. Where did the abduction take place?"

"In Houston." Alonsa seldom talked to anyone about the abduction anymore, though it had been all she could talk about for the first year. But tonight the memories were razor sharp and the need to put them into words was suddenly all-consuming.

"Give me a minute to check on Brandon," she said, "and I'll tell you about it." She paused. "But I should warn you. I still can't talk about it without getting upset."

"I have a broad shoulder, great for collecting tears."

"I'll try not to drench you."

Brandon was curled up in a soft knit throw, laughing at the DVD he'd seen dozens of times, apparently with no repercussions from his fall. She watched him for a moment, letting the reassurance of his safety sink into her troubled soul. She knew she was overprotective with him, but how could she not be under the circumstances?

Hawk was sitting at the table when she returned. She refilled both their coffee cups and joined him. It was more caffeine than she normally drank this late at night, but there was little chance she'd sleep anyway.

"Are you sure you want to hear this, Hawk? It's not as if talking about it changes anything."

"It could, if talk leads to the right action."

He only thought that because he didn't know the whole story. For that matter, neither did she. She thought back, trying to find a place to begin.

"It was five weeks to the day after my husband had been killed in New York. I buried him here in Dobbin and decided to stay on with the kids through the winter. I thought a change of scenery might help us all handle things better."

"Makes sense."

"I thought so at the time. My mistake. Everyone here was friendly and went out of their way to welcome us, but the only one I'd really connected with was Cutter's Aunt Merlee. She'd taken me under her wing. Have you met her yet?"

"No, but I've heard about her. Linney adores her."

"Everyone adores her. Anyway, that weekend she'd invited me and the children to visit her in her Houston townhouse so that I could take Lucy to some of the museums and child-oriented activities without having to make the long drive back to Dobbin at the end of the day. Brandon was only a year old and fussy that day, so Merlee had offered to watch him while Lucy and I took in the zoo."

"So it was just the two of you?"

"Yes, mother-and-daughter time and Lucy was thrilled that she wouldn't have to share me. Between the trauma of Todd's death, the move and taking care of Brandon, I'd given her far too little of myself."

"It must have been a hard time for all of you."

It was still a hard time, all but unbearable on nights like this, with the sound of that voice on the phone echoing through her senses.

Keep talking, Alonsa. Get through this. You should be able to talk of it without falling completely apart. It's been two years.

Her mind fixated on the events of that heartbreaking day, and she found small solace in remembering her daughter's enthusiasm and laughter. "Lucy loved all the animals, but the sea lions were her favorite. It was nearing two when I told her we needed to go back to Merlee's. She begged to see the sea lions one more time. I gave in, of course."

If she hadn't… No. Going over the ifs didn't help. The counselor had worked for months to get her to move beyond that and the personal recriminations. She took a deep breath and exhaled slowly.

"While we were watching the sea lion antics, a large school group arrived and we were inundated by first and second graders. Someone pushed someone and a fight broke out. A little girl was shoved to the ground and started wailing. I went to help her up while the teachers stopped the fight. When I looked for Lucy, she wasn't there.

"I wasn't worried when I first lost sight of her, but then after minutes passed and I couldn't locate her among the children, I started to panic." Alonsa's voice grew shaky.

Hawk stood and rounded the table, resting his hands on her shoulders. "Maybe tonight's not the best time for this. Why don't you get some rest, and I'll come back tomorrow morning?"

"I'm okay." His touch and sympathy were disconcerting in the quiet kitchen. "Do you have children, Hawk?"

"No. I was married for a while once, but no kids.

I'm sure I can't begin to understand what you're going though."

Yet he was here and a good listener. Or else the pain was just so overwhelming tonight she had to have the release of talking about it.

"I haven't seen my daughter since that day at the zoo. All I get is the phone calls, the torment of her voice asking for me when I can't go to her."

"Surely the investigation uncovered some leads."

"None that produced results."

"Exactly what does the recorded voice say when you get the phone calls?"

"It's a young girl's voice. All she says is 'Mommy' and then there's a click and the call disconnects. Craig doubts that it's Lucy's voice. He thinks it's more likely some sick pervert who heard about the case at the time and gets his kicks torturing me."

"Who's Craig?"

"Craig Dalliers, the FBI agent who's heading up the kidnapping investigation. He's been on the case almost since the beginning."

"Who conducted the initial search for Lucy, the local police or the FBI?"

"Both. The police started the process, but the FBI took over as soon as they got clearance. My husband Todd was an FBI agent killed in the line of duty."

"I didn't realize that."

"How could you know?" Alonsa asked. "We've barely met."

Yet here she was pouring out her soul to him in her kitchen. She was still wearing the blue cocktail dress she'd pulled from the back of her closet. He was in his tux. The bizarreness of the situation struck her and she wondered what she'd been thinking to invite him in when he'd driven her home. Still, she gave him the details of the search as succinctly as possible.

Hawk stepped away and started to pace. "What's going on with the search now?"

"The FBI has assured me the case is still active."

"What exactly does that mean?"

"I'm not sure. I haven't had an update in over three months."

"Do they think the kidnapping was a revenge crime related to someone your husband arrested?"

"They did at first. Now Craig believes it was probably random."

"What do you think?"

"I trust Craig's judgment. I have no reason not to. He worked with Todd on a daily basis. Only..."

Only Craig, and the agents he'd assigned to help with the case, hadn't found Lucy. The growing doubts she'd tried to deny crowded her mind. Craig had his faults, especially in the personal morals department, but he was a capable agent. Even Todd admitted that.

Hawk stopped pacing and straddled a chair next to hers. "I'd like to talk to the agent heading up the investigation."

"Why?"

"Sometimes a fresh mind and viewpoint can help."

"I wish I believed that, but there's nothing to view."

"No one disappears without a trace, Alonsa."

But Lucy had. If there was a lead, the FBI would have found it. Having Hawk talk to Craig wouldn't change anything and would likely just aggravate Craig and stop him from assigning the case to a top agent.

"I'm sorry, but the FBI is handling the case and I don't see how your talking to them can possibly help."

"It can't hurt. A new person can spot mistakes a lot faster than the guy who's made them."

The comment provoked her. Hawk only knew the little she'd told him. He hadn't been here through the months of anguish, hadn't gone through the agony of building up hope with every minuscule lead only to have it blow up in her face. He didn't have a clue how deeply involved Craig and his team had been in the case.

She tapped her fingers on the table's edge. "Why would you assume they've made mistakes?"

"They haven't found your daughter."

"And you think you can?"

"Yeah. I do."

This discussion had crossed a dozen lines she hadn't seen coming. Did this man she barely knew really expect her to hire him to search for Lucy? A dull throb started at the back of her skull. Her stomach rolled.

The whole idea was ludicrous. Then again, what did she have to lose, other than her sanity, if she gathered hope again only to have it dissolve into emptiness? Or if she failed to give Brandon any kind of normal life because she was caught up in a revived investigation that would tear her apart on a daily basis.

And then there were the financial considerations. Hawk worked for Cutter and she was certain their services didn't come cheap. A private investigation would require money she didn't have because she'd already spent a large portion of Todd's insurance on traveling the country that first year, putting up flyers and appearing on every TV station and talk-radio program that would let her plead for information about her missing child.

Yet if there was even a ghost of a chance…

She raised her eyes and met Hawk's dark penetrating gaze. Something seemed to give way, as if the cords holding her together were beginning to fray.

"Exactly what are you suggesting, Hawk?"

"That I conduct my own investigation into Lucy's disappearance. That you give me full access to any and all information you have or can get from the FBI. That you work with me and answer every question honestly. That you have a little faith in my ability."

"And if you don't find her?"

"You'll be no worse off than you are now."

And if he succeeded, she'd have Lucy home again. Unless… The possibilities swelled inside her and her breath burned as if she were inhaling pure acid. They'd found no trace of Lucy, but that had let her maintain the hope that Lucy was alive. What if she wasn't? What if she'd died at the hands of some pervert? Could Alonsa bear knowing the certainty of that?

Hawk reached across the space between them and took her hands in his. "I realize you know nothing about me, Alonsa, that you have no reason to trust me, but you can talk to Cutter. He'll vouch that I have a talent for smoking out facts where none seem to exist. I'm not bragging. It's just how it is."

Not bragging. Not arrogant. Just sure of himself. It went with the Special Ops territory, she suspected. It was his reason for being so quick to want to jump into this that she couldn't decipher. And there was still the cost.

"Even if I want to hire you, I'm not sure I can afford you."

"You won't have to pay anything except reasonable expenses. An economy flight from time to time. A cheap hotel when the need arises. Frogmen aren't used to first class."

"You can't work for nothing."

"I can do what I want for now. Once I start the new assignment with Cutter my time for this will be limited, but I can move on this full speed until then. So the sooner we rev the engines, the better."

He had answered all her questions but one. "Why, Hawk? Why would you do this for a virtual stranger?"

"I like the way you dance. And it's the right thing to do."

HAWK TOOK THE LONG way back to the Double M. Scenes from the past pummeled his mind as he drove the dark meandering roads through lonesome strands of pine. Flying over enemy territory searching for a fellow frogman who hadn't returned from a mission. Swimming beneath the current with the body of a fallen buddy strapped to him like a second skin.

No man left behind.

He'd lived by that vow in the ragged mountains of Afghanistan and in Middle Eastern deserts so hot he'd felt as if his blood were boiling. Now he was back in America and out of uniform, but the vow seemed no less important. A little girl torn from her mother and dragged into who knew what. Didn't Alonsa deserve to find her daughter or at least get some kind of closure?

A major concern right now was just how much of this was about him and what he needed. He'd been out of the service for months now and still he hadn't found any kind of groove. That's why he'd joined up with Cutter.

Becoming a SEAL had made him part of a team that tackled everything that was thrown at them with never a thought of failure. No one had been more surprised than he was to discover how much he missed being a part of that team and of something bigger than himself.

The only real drawback to taking on this case was the sizzling attraction that had hit the first moment he'd laid eyes on Alonsa. The way she'd moved on the dance floor. The way she'd felt in his arms when they two-stepped their way through the sultry country-western ballad. The way she'd looked in that chair, with her legs curled up under her. Even the way she'd poured him a cup of coffee.

Hell, everything about her turned him on.

But seducing her was not in the rules of engagement. It would make him less effective, might even complicate their relationship to the point where working together would become impossible. Worse, it would be taking advantage of her weakest vulnerability.

He'd just have to keep his libido under control, at least until the job was done. That would require seeing her without touching her on a regular basis and going home to cold showers and an empty bed every night.

And he'd thought the war zone was tough.

ALONSA RINSED BRANDON'S empty cereal bowl, placed it in the dishwasher and poured herself a glass of orange juice. She'd lain awake for most of the night, tossing, turning and vacillating between enthusiasm for Hawk's offer and a dread that was pitted deep in her soul. A dread that made no sense.

She wanted her daughter back with every fiber of her being, prayed for it perpetually, had spent an entire year so consumed with finding her that she'd sinfully neglected her son. The belief that Lucy was still alive and that someday they'd be reunited was the glue that held her together.

But what if Lucy wasn't?

"Mom, come see what I built."

"Okay, sweetie. I'll be right there." She took her juice and ambled to the family room where Brandon had arranged his wooden blocks in a tower that reached his chin.

"It's a skyscraped."

"Skyscraper," she corrected him. "A super-duper one."

He laughed and knocked it over, scattering the blocks in every direction.

"All that work just to watch it fall?"

"Yeah. It's fun."

The hum of an engine in her drive sent a new wave of apprehension slithering along her nerve endings. She went to the front window and watched as Hawk climbed from behind the wheel and started for the house.

Amazingly he looked even more virile than he had last night. His jeans were worn, his shirt a black, collarless knit that hugged his hard frame, not the Western type so many of the local ranchers wore. But the boots and black Stetson insured that genuine, rugged cowboy look.

Yet something set him apart from the other men in the area. Maybe it was the cocky swagger or the determined set of his chin. And suddenly she knew why the apprehension had taken such hold of her.

Hawk was battlefield-hardened and success-proven. If he set out to do something, it wasn't likely he'd stop until he succeeded. This time that determination would be directed full force at investigating her daughter's disappearance. She'd finally get answers. She'd find out what happened to Lucy.

But what if the truth was more than her heart could bear?

Her fingers were clammy and her heart was in her throat when she opened the door and ushered him inside.

Chapter Three

Hawk had slept little last night. Nothing unusual for him. When his mind was in gear, his body seemed to refuel on adrenaline. It was that way for most of the frogmen he knew. Maybe that was what set them apart, a trait that had helped them make it through the initial BUD/S training and later take dangerous missions in stride.

In the early hours of the morning, his surge of energy had pushed him through an extensive online search for information on Todd Salatoya. The basic facts were easy enough to locate for someone who knew how to maneuver the intricate maze of informational sites. What Hawk hadn't been able to find on his own, Cutter's tech guy Eduardo had sniffed out for him. Actually, he'd waited until seven to call Eduardo. He figured some men slept.

Todd had had an exemplary record as an FBI agent, highly acclaimed. He'd been killed in the line of duty just as Alonsa had said, shot repeatedly by a drug dealer manning an AK-47. It had apparently been a brutal clash in a sting that Todd had masterminded. This time he'd made a few fatal misjudgments and the cartel had been waiting for him.

So Todd Salatoya went down on a bitterly cold winter night and never went home to his beautiful wife and two kids. Merely weeks later his daughter had been abducted from the Houston Zoo.

In spite of Craig's insistence to the contrary, it was highly possible that the two were related—a payback against Todd's family or a warning to other agents not to mess with the cartel. If so, Hawk might be about to open a load of trouble for himself and, worse, for Alonsa.

His insides tightened as he took the short walk from his truck to Alonsa's front door. This definitely wasn't what he'd expected when he'd driven Alonsa home last night. Then he'd been a man following his libido. Not that he'd be able to just turn off his sexual urges where she was concerned. Some men claimed they could. Hawk figured they lied.

What went on in the hormonal realm was beyond his control. What he did about that attraction was what mattered here. Hawk was a champion in the behavioral control game, which was why he wouldn't try to jump Alonsa's bones.

In the meantime, he had plenty to focus on. If there was even a chance that little girl was still alive, she needed to be returned to her mother. He'd play this as if she were alive and that any wrong move could work against finding her.

Alonsa opened the door before he knocked. She was dressed in jeans and a sweater the color of the Caribbean Sea. Her long dark hair was pulled into a knot at the back of her head with long silky strands left to hang loose and dance about her shoulders. She wore no apparent makeup but her full lips were soft and glossy. Her dark lashes curved above her bewitching eyes.

Reel it in, Hawk. This is strictly business.

IT WAS THE FIRST TIME in a year that Alonsa had been forced to go over the details of her husband's death, though it had never stopped haunting her. Still, she described the events to Hawk as precisely as possible.

Hawk listened without interruption until she'd run out of emotional steam and sank back in the big overstuffed chair by the window. She kicked off her leather slides and curled her left foot up in the chair with her.

"What I know about that night came from Craig. Before Todd's death, I never knew much about what he actually did," she admitted reluctantly.

"Is that because it was classified?"

"Partly, but we had decided early in the marriage that the less I knew about the danger he dealt with the better."

"Makes sense."

Actually they'd quit communicating about much of anything except the children those last few months, but no reason to go into that with Hawk.

"Were most of his assignments in the New York area?"

"No. He was frequently gone for months at a time."

"That must have been hard on the marriage."

"I stayed busy," she said, avoiding a direct answer. Busy with her children. They'd spent hours at the park. Lucy had loved the park. She maneuvered the climbing apparatus better than the older kids and almost never fell. Once she...

Alonsa reined in the thoughts as pain threaded itself through the membranes of her heart.

"Maybe we should take a break," Hawk said, obviously recognizing the signs of a woman about to crater on him.

She nodded her agreement. "I need to check on Brandon. I worry when he's too quiet. There's no end to what a curious three-year-old can get into."

She stretched to her feet, but didn't bother to slip back into her shoes. Her bright teal socks mocked her gray mood as she padded to the small play alcove just off the kitchen.

Originally the space had held a large farmhouse table surrounded by tall wooden chairs and benches. But she'd needed Brandon close to her, constantly in her sight for the first year after Lucy's abduction. Even now, she liked having him nearby so that she heard him immediately if he called out to her.

Brandon had given up on building towers and had constructed a ranch with his blocks and plastic animals, complete with a riding arena for the toy horses Linney had bought him. Carne was gnawing on a short length of rope. The well-chewed, soggy knot was his favorite toy.

"Would you like a juice box?" she asked.

"Cherry." Brandon sat one of his cowboys on top of a horse. "Can I have a cookie, too?"

"Sure. One cookie and some juice coming up."

"I want to go outside and ride my tractor."

"As soon as my guest leaves."

"Make him go home now."

"We still have things to talk about."

"Talk to me, Mommy. Outside."

He should probably be outside playing with kids his own age. Even Merlee had suggested Alonsa enroll him in the preschool program at church for at least a few days a week. Alonsa had gotten as far as registering him, but on the morning she was to drop him off, she discovered the class was going on a field trip to a local pumpkin patch.

If she could lose Lucy when they were one-on-one at the zoo, how could a teacher possibly watch Brandon close enough in a group of children? She'd taken him home and given up on the preschool idea altogether.

Brandon and Carne followed her back to the kitchen. Hawk helped himself to a refill of coffee as she handed Brandon his juice. Carne dropped the chew toy from his mouth and made a task of watching Hawk.

It hit Alonsa how strange it was to have a man making himself at home in her kitchen. It should have been more awkward than it was, but Hawk had an easy way about him that made her comfortable. And a blatant virility that had the opposite effect.

"Wanna ride my tractor," Brandon said, directing the comment at Hawk and letting a few crumbles of cookie tumble from the corners of his mouth.

"Remember the rule," Alonsa reminded him. "Don't talk with your mouth full. And I told you Mr. Taylor and I have business to discuss."

"You have a tractor?" Hawk said. "Awesome."

"It goes fast, too."

"I'd like to see it." Hawk glanced at Alonsa. "If it's okay with your mother."

"She don't care, huh, Mom?" He didn't wait for an answer, but started running toward the back door.

"Get your windbreaker," she called after him.

"Aww." Nonetheless, he followed orders and yanked a bright red jacket from a low hook by the mudroom door.

Alonsa retrieved her cell phone from the counter next to the cookie jar and clipped it to the waistband of her jeans. "I suppose we can talk as well outside as in, as long as we stay out of Brandon's earshot," she said.

"I don't see why not. I could use a little fresh air myself."

Alonsa wasn't quite sure how to take that. Was it her house in particular Hawk found stifling or houses in general? Not that it mattered. She detoured to the family room for her shoes then followed the both of them outside and into the bright sunshine that characterized living in this part of Texas. It was January, and at midmorning the temperature had already climbed into the high fifties.

"It's snowing in New York," she said, thinking out loud.

"Do you miss that?" Hawk asked.

"Not often."

"Broadway?"

"Sometimes," she admitted. "And the city in general." Her quiet life in Texas seemed a galaxy away from the life she'd once lived.

Brandon, on the other hand, knew only this life. He didn't remember his father or his sister. He knew only what Alonsa had shared with him and what he'd seen in the many photographs scattered about the house. His father had died while being a hero. His sister was away.

Occasionally he asked questions about Lucy, but for the most part the simple explanation that she would be home soon satisfied him. At some point she'd have to tell him the truth, but not yet.

He jumped on his battery-operated tractor, turned the key and started bouncing down the blacktop driveway. "Watch me go fast, Mr. Taylor."

"Don't get a speeding ticket."

Brandon laughed and aimed for a bumpy spot in the drive with Carne running in front of him, his yappy bark colliding with the caw of a belligerent crow.

"Don't go past the curve," Alonsa called. "Stay where I can see you."

"Don't you ever let him outside alone?" Hawk asked.

"In the fenced backyard, where I can watch him from the kitchen window."

"That's it?"

"He's only three, Hawk. And we're not that far off the highway. Anyone could wander up."

"It's half a mile to the cattle gap. Ranching kids get used to wide-open spaces early."

"It's not like I have him imprisoned. He has a play set with a slide, swings, a fort and a huge sandbox to play with his construction equipment."

She walked away, heading to an old tire swing that dangled from the low branch of an oak in the side yard. She didn't have to explain her child-rearing habits to Hawk Taylor. Besides, Brandon wasn't a ranching kid. They didn't have a single cow on the land.

Hawk followed her. He leaned against the trunk of

the tree while she stirred the dirt beneath the swing with the toes of her shoes. Squirrels darted among the branches over her head. A light breeze crackled the dried, fallen leaves. Brandon's tractor rumbled in the background, punctuated by Carne's excited barks.

Life was going on as usual, only nothing felt usual today. Tension swelled between her and Hawk, not quite anger, not quite attraction, but some weird place in the middle.

He wrapped his fingers around an overhead branch. His muscles flexed and pushed at the cotton fabric of his shirt. "You're not convinced Lucy's abduction was random, are you?"

She exhaled slowly. "I told you that Craig Dalliers says all the evidence points to the fact that it was. The FBI has thoroughly checked out and eliminated every possibility that it was related to Todd's work with the agency."

"So you've said. That wasn't the question."

So he'd read the signs, picked up on the fact that if she'd been fully convinced Lucy's kidnapping was random, she wouldn't be so squeamish about letting Brandon out of her sight for even a second.

"I haven't ruled out anything," she admitted.

"And yet you've remained here in Dobbin, where you were living when the abduction took place, instead of losing yourself back in the crowded city you claim to miss so much. Why is that?"

He wasn't the first to question that, though most people hadn't put as much thought into the situation as Hawk clearly had. Usually she brushed the question off. She'd never get away with that with Hawk.

"Lucy knew her phone number and her address. If

she ever remembers, if she tries to get in touch with us, I want to be here. I know it gets more doubtful that will happen after two years, but that was my reasoning in the beginning."

"And now?"

"I like my work and the house is paid for."

Hawk swatted absently at a horsefly that had settled on his arm. "Have you given more thought to setting up a meeting between me and Craig Dalliers?"

"I'll give him a call later and see what I can work out."

"What's wrong with now? Or give me his direct number and I'll call him."

"I should talk to him first."

"So that you can try to justify why I'm getting in on the case?"

"Yes," she admitted. "I don't want him to think I doubt his abilities. He's given the case his all. I don't want to seem ungrateful."

"No problem. Handle Craig any way you want," Hawk said. "As long as you let him know I expect his full cooperation in supplying me with all the facts. Anything less will sabotage my investigation."

"I'll make sure he understands."

"And then I'd like us to take a trip together to the zoo this afternoon. I want to see the exact spot where you were standing when Lucy disappeared."

Back to the zoo. Back into the depths of the setting where the nightmare had started. A numbness settled in her mind. She got out of the swing. Her legs went weak.

Hawk wrapped his strong hands around her forearms, literally holding her up. "I know this will be hard on you, Alonsa, but it's important. And I'll be there with you every second."

"I don't see how it can help."

"I need to see the paths in and away from the area so I'll get a better understanding of how someone could lure a little girl from her mother in a crowd of people with no one noticing."

New fears surfaced. "I don't want to take Brandon there."

"Don't you trust me to keep him safe?"

"I don't trust myself not to break down and I don't want him there to witness that."

"I thought you might feel that way. I talked to Linney this morning. She's agreed to watch him."

"Do you always think of everything?"

"Part of the SEAL creed."

"Along with holding women together when they're falling apart?"

"Only the hot ones. You qualify, but you won't fall apart. Just hang tough."

"Tough, that's me." She took a deep breath and struggled to will the strength he thought she had into her body and soul. "I guess I should go ahead and call Craig since you're ready to start working the case."

"Excellent idea. I'll keep an eye on the boy for you."

She heard Brandon calling to him to watch him ride the second she turned to walk away.

She felt as if she'd just signed on for a ride herself and her insides were rattling like the child-size tractor. The difference was the tractor was on familiar turf.

Alonsa was in the hands of a stranger, a cowboy war

hero with enough self-assurance to take on the world—or one missing child. The test would be to see if Hawk Taylor was as good as he claimed. And if she could survive the Houston Zoo.

ALONSA MADE THE CALL to Craig. He was unavailable but she'd left a message for him to call at once. He hadn't as yet.

They arrived at the zoo just after one in the afternoon. Alonsa's legs felt leaden as they made their way to the saltwater pool at the edge of the main plaza. The facility wasn't crowded and the attendance appeared to be mostly young mothers and nannies enjoying a day out in the sunshine with their preschoolers. It was probably too soon after Christmas break for an overload of school field trips.

Alonsa spotted a boy about Brandon's age lolling behind and ignoring his mother's pleas to keep up with her and the twins she was pushing in a double stroller. She fought the urge to stop and caution the mother about what could happen if she let her son out of her sight.

She'd done that the first year after Lucy's disappearance, initiated herself in any situation that made her nervous. For the most part people had reacted to the intrusion with indifference or downright hostility. Eventually, she'd stopped monitoring everyone's parenting skills.

Her heart hammered in her chest as they reached the dreaded exhibit. She stopped, her feet rooted to the earth. Two years fell away and she slid back in time to the day she'd stood here with Lucy squealing in delight at the antics of the fascinating creatures. A shudder ripped through her.

Hawk reached for her hand. Hers was clammy, but still she held on to his.

"Hang in here with me, Alonsa. This won't take long. Just give me a recap. Where were you standing? What did you notice?"

"Okay." Her voice felt as if it were pushing through layers of rough wool. "We were standing near the rail, there next to that sign that describes the animals. I read it to Lucy. Even at four she was starting to read and was interested in all the informational material."

Highly intelligent. Great swimmers. Could hold their breath for extended periods of time. Bizarrely, the facts, if not the exact words, swam through the fog clouding Alonsa's mind.

"There was a woman standing near us with her husband and several children. They were on vacation and had driven down from Ohio. We talked."

"Did you notice anything suspicious about her?" Hawk asked. "Did she ask unusual questions or touch Lucy in a familiar manner?"

"No. They were just nice, friendly people. Craig tracked them down and talked with her during the first days of the investigation. She cooperated fully, but she hadn't seen Lucy leave the area."

"Do you remember anyone else in the area before the group of schoolchildren arrived?"

"There were other people around, but no one else registered in my mind. Believe me, I tried to remember everything and I answered hundreds of questions right after Lucy disappeared. There were no suspicious instances or people."

"Did you talk to anyone else that day or notice the same people standing around at different exhibits?"

"The only person I had a real conversation with was one of the workers. We were near the panda exhibit and she was nice enough to answer all of Lucy's questions. She was a college student working during her summer break."

"Do you remember her name?"

"Elle Carrigan. Both Craig and I talked to her after the abduction. She didn't see Lucy again once we'd walked away from her."

No one knew anything, and Alonsa was starting to think working with Hawk on this was a big mistake. There would be nothing he could do but cross the same *T*'s and dot the identical *I*'s that Craig had already crossed and dotted.

Hawk squeezed her hand as if reading her misgivings. His strength seeped into her. When she looked up she was gripped by the intensity of his stare as he studied the surroundings. He was committed and doing his job. She was the liability here.

"I'll be fine, Hawk. I'll stand right here. You do what you need to do. Search every aspect of the area."

"Are you sure?"

"I'm sure."

She stood at the railing, watching but not really seeing the sea lions. There were three now. There had been only two when she'd stood here with Lucy. Cali and Kamia, both females. Lucy had said she was going to name one of her dolls Cali. She'd never seen her dolls again.

"Mrs. Salatoya."

Alonsa turned, startled. She recognized Elle Carrigan immediately. "Elle. I didn't expect to see you here today."

"I graduated in December. I'm working at the zoo full-time now."

"That's great."

"I'm glad I ran into you. I'd been thinking about trying to find your phone number so I could call you to see if the photo was any help in the investigation."

Alonsa failed to make sense of the comment. "What photo?"

"The one I sent to the FBI."

"I haven't heard anything about a photo. Was this recently?"

"A few months ago. It was the strangest thing. I was going through some photos that belonged to my sister when I noticed this kid that looked exactly like Lucy. I even recognized the T-shirt she'd worn the day I met her. The one with the silly turtle on it. I commented on it at the time. Remember?"

"I remember. Tell me about the photo."

"Tonya—that's my younger sister—was clowning around with her friends near the gate and waiting on me to finish my shift at three o'clock. Anyway, there was a lady and a little girl in the background of one of the pictures they snapped."

"You're sure it was Lucy?"

"Almost positive."

"And she was with a lady?"

"Yes, the lady was turned so that you couldn't see her face, but she was holding Lucy's hand and leading her through the exit gate."

Alonsa's chest constricted. A woman leaving the

zoo with Lucy. This was the first she'd heard of this. "Are you certain the FBI received the photo?"

"I sent it to Craig Dalliers and he called in person to thank me for the lead."

"Did he say it was Lucy in the photo?"

"I asked, but he said he couldn't comment on the authenticity."

Lucy had walked out of the zoo with a woman. They had the suspect's picture. Yet Craig hadn't even called her. Did he believe the girl in the photo wasn't Lucy? Was he following up on the lead?

"I hope they find Lucy soon," Elle said.

Alonsa only nodded, her ability to converse swallowed up in the sensations coursing through her. She scanned the area for Hawk. When she caught his eye, she waved him over, then turned back to Elle. "There's someone I want you to meet. He's conducting a private investigation into Lucy's disappearance. That's why I'm here today."

She'd just finished making the introductions and explaining the photo to Hawk when her cell phone vibrated in her jacket pocket. She checked the caller ID. Craig Dalliers, returning her call. The timing couldn't have been better.

"I have to take this," she said, stepping away from Elle and Hawk so that they wouldn't hear her phone conversation. Her anger toward Craig spiked into jagged peaks. How dare he keep a development like this from her.

Chapter Four

"Why didn't you tell me about the photo?" The words tumbled out of Alonsa's mouth in a rush of frustration.

"Which photo?"

"The one of Lucy being led away from the zoo."

Her question was met with silence. "It was Lucy in the photo, wasn't it?"

"Yes," Craig admitted. "It was Lucy, but you need to stay calm, Alonsa. I can explain everything."

"And you darn well will. Why didn't you call me?"

"I was waiting for an opportune time to talk to you."

"You got the photo months ago."

"I didn't want to get into this with you over the phone. I'd planned to come to Texas as soon as I got a chance and show you the picture in person. Not that it changes anything."

"How can you say that? It means we know that Lucy was abducted by a woman and not some sick perverted male. That changes a few things for me. I live on hope, Craig. I've lived on nothing else for two years. What else have you kept from me?"

"Nothing. How did you find out about the photo?"

"From Elle Carrigan."

"Tell me you are not still trying to investigate this on your own."

"No. Not on my own. I've hired a private investigator." Her bitterness over having been kept in the dark about the photo made telling him about Hawk a lot easier. She didn't have to justify anything.

"That is a ludicrous waste of money and you know it," Craig sputtered. "No private investigator has the resources the FBI does. No one else is going to give this case the attention I have. I've supervised a lot of it myself and assigned some of my top men to assist."

"And all of you ignored the photograph of Lucy and the abductor."

"I haven't ignored it, Alonsa. The photo doesn't show anything of the abductor but the back of her head. All we know now that we didn't know before is that a woman was involved."

"You should have called me," she insisted. "I have a right to know."

"I'm checking every lead, Alonsa, including the photo. You know how I feel about you, how I've always felt about you. I was right there with you through the worst of this. You cried in my arms and I cried with you. Do you think some high-priced private investigator is going to stick by you the way I have or care about you and Lucy the way I do?"

Her anger subsided. Craig had been there since the beginning and had put in lots of hours. He'd personally been involved in every aspect those first critical months, staying in Houston for several weeks. Perhaps she had been hasty and grasping at straws in hiring Hawk.

She turned so that Hawk was directly in her line of vision. She studied his profile, his muscular physique, his broad shoulders, the confident stance. The way Elle was hanging on his every word, clearly drawn to him by the pure magnetism of his virility and personality, the way Alonsa had seen every other woman react to him.

"What kind of expertise does this new investigator bring to the table, or has he just sold you a bill of goods?" Craig asked, putting words to her doubts.

Hawk turned toward her as she contemplated the question, his piercing eyes capturing her gaze. An intensity that defied description punctuated their dark depths. It was that intensity she was staking her hopes on, not his good looks.

"I appreciate all you've done, Craig, but I've made up my mind. Mr. Taylor and I would like to meet with you so that you can fill him in on what's been done and explain exactly where you are in the search."

"I can't release confidential FBI files."

"This is my daughter we're talking about. If you have anything that will help me find her, I should have it."

"You know I'll do what I can to help, but for the record, I think you're making a big mistake."

"You've made that clear."

"I'll look at my schedule, try to rearrange what I have to do and see if I can get a flight to Houston later in the week."

"Hold on a second." She walked over to where Hawk and Elle were standing and covered the phone's mike with her hand. "I'm talking to Craig. He says he can fly to Houston later in the week. Does that work for you?"

"How about if we fly to New York tomorrow and meet with him?"

"I'll have to take Brandon or find someone to leave him with."

"Either way. The sooner I get all the prelim facts, the sooner we can put together a search-and-recovery plan of action."

A plan of action to find her daughter. It was just words, but still it ignited a new spark of optimism. She put the phone back to her ear. "We'll be in New York tomorrow, Craig. I'll call once I make flight reservations and let you know what time we'll be available."

"That's a push for my schedule, but we'll set something up, maybe over dinner."

"I'd prefer the meeting be in your office."

Her resolve hardened now that the initial hurdle had passed. She and Hawk Taylor would be traveling to New York. For the first time in over a year, the search was actively moving forward. She had Hawk to thank for that.

ALONSA STRETCHED BENEATH the sheet and light blanket, staring at the whirling blades of the ceiling fan. The fan wasn't really needed this time of year, but she depended on the soft whir to lull her into sleep. Most nights it worked.

It should have tonight. Everything had fallen into place. Cutter's Aunt Merlee was visiting the Double M this week and she'd been genuinely delighted at the prospect of helping Linney babysit Brandon. He was excited about seeing the horses. They'd even invited Carne along.

Alonsa had been fortunate enough to book direct flights at halfway reasonable rates departing from George Bush Intercontinental at 9:10 a.m. Her Marriott points allowed her to book a five-star hotel within walking distance of Craig's office. Only the weather wasn't cooperating. The weather channel was predicting sleet and possible snow in New York by afternoon.

She missed the city in many ways, yet she dreaded walking the familiar streets again. Her memories of the city were all tied up with her memories of Lucy.

Tomorrow she'd return to the city with Hawk Taylor. That in itself should make the trip even more traumatic for her. Oddly, it was having the opposite effect.

Watching Hawk at the party the other night, she'd been put off by the way women had so eagerly succumbed to his charms. His flagrant virility, rugged good looks and devastating smile had them practically swooning.

She'd discovered a different and far more impressive side of him over the last two days.

Everyone who heard about Lucy's disappearance had offered condolences and their willingness to help in any way they could. Hawk had been the only one who'd actually backed up that offer with direct action.

Not that the others hadn't meant well. It was just that Hawk had some added dimension to him, a strength of purpose and determination that defied the odds. It was as if he was wired for action.

She'd never keep up with him tomorrow if she didn't get some sleep tonight. She rolled onto her side, took deep breaths and began silently chanting a yoga mantra. Finally her mind drifted into indistinct shadows and her eyelids grew heavy.

The jangling ring of the phone on her bedside table practically sent her into orbit. She reached for it, then hesitated. No one called her this late. If this was another tormenting reminder of Lucy's sweet voice, she didn't think she could take it.

The caller ID said Craig Dalliers. She pounded her pillow in a rush of frustration and picked up the receiver and grumbled a greeting.

"Is that you, Alonsa?"

His voice slurred. He'd been drinking. That explained the late call. Whiskey brought out the worst in him. "Do you know what time it is?"

"You're grumpy. Were you busy?"

"It's midnight, Craig. I'm in bed."

"Alone?"

"Of course. Brandon has his own room. He's—" She realized then he hadn't been referring to Brandon. The question was too far over the line to warrant an answer. "Do you have news about Lucy, because there's no other reason for you to be calling me this time of night?"

"No news."

"I need to get some sleep, Craig. I'll see you tomorrow. We can discuss whatever you're calling about then."

"Right. You're coming to see me and bringing some cowboy detective who's convinced you he can do what the whole damn FBI can't."

"This isn't a territorial battle between him and the Bureau. I'm just trying to get Lucy back."

"That's what you have me for. You should trust me. You should have listened to me when I warned you about Todd. You weren't the first woman whose life he destroyed."

His voice slurred more. The guy was more inebriated than she'd thought. He must be in a bar somewhere. "Go home, Craig, but take a cab or call Ginny to come and pick you up."

"Ginny's at her mother's."

"Then call a cab. Good night." She hung up before he had time to continue the conversation or go off in another direction. Whatever he said tonight under the influence, he'd likely be sorry for tomorrow. Even if he wasn't, she would be.

Unfortunately she was wide awake again. She snuggled beneath the covers, but one of Craig's annoying questions became a niggling deterrent to sleep.

Are you alone?

Very alone in her king-size bed, the same way she'd been for two years. Her emotions had been too raw after Todd's death and Lucy's disappearance to even think of a man in a sexual way. She still didn't need a man.

Yet she'd felt something the other night when her gaze had first locked with Hawk's. She'd blamed it on the champagne, but he was too much a man not to affect her on a sensual level.

But a slight stirring of sensual attraction was normal. It just meant she was still alive. She'd make sure it went no further than that.

It took Hawk less than five minutes to realize that Craig Dalliers had no intention of cooperating fully with him. This was his baby, and he had no interest in throwing it into the private sector.

Craig had the power seat behind his desk. Alonsa and

Hawk sat in uncomfortable straight-backed chairs facing him. So far they'd covered the introductions and greetings and not much more.

Craig was throwing around his importance, telling them about his recent promotion and how he'd specified to his superiors that he remain in charge of the investigation into Lucy's disappearance.

Hawk wasn't impressed. Bureaucracy and formalities bored him. That was the one part of the military he'd had enough of. He was about to ask Craig to get on with the show when Alonsa beat him to it.

"I want to see the photograph Elle Carrigan sent you."

"Technically, Tonya Carrigan sent the snapshot. It was taken with her camera," Craig said.

Alonsa leaned forward. "I want to see it."

Craig nodded and reached for a manila folder from a stack of similar ones on the back of his desk. He opened it slowly and pulled out a 4 x 6 color glossy. He shrugged and his lips slanted into tight lines of resignation as he walked to the front of his desk and handed the photo to Alonsa.

Her muscles visibly bunched and her right hand shook as she reached for it. She fixated on the image and then put a hand to her head as if she needed the support to hold it up.

"It's definitely Lucy," Alonsa said, her voice tremulous.

"I know, and I was trying to avoid putting you through this," Craig said.

She continued to study the photograph. "I don't understand why she'd walk away with that woman. She had to know I'd be looking for her." Alonsa handed the photograph to Hawk.

The child's profile was distinct. Even Hawk recognized her as Lucy from the many framed photos he'd seen of her in Alonsa's house.

There was nothing of the woman but her back. She had on fitted jeans and a pale pink knit shirt. A nice figure. Slightly longer than shoulder length blond hair that hung straight until it curled a bit on the ends. No way to accurately judge her age, but the hairdo and dress suggested youth. No older than thirty-five, he'd estimate.

Lucy looked a bit upset but not hysterical the way you'd expect from a girl being abducted in the bright light of day. It was possible she'd gotten lost and asked for help. She might have believed the woman was taking her to Alonsa.

But what was the chance that a random woman visiting the zoo in the broad light of day would take a lost little girl as an opportunity for a kidnapping, especially when she'd never asked for a ransom?

"Maybe the woman was hired by the drug cartel that killed Todd," Alonsa speculated.

"We've covered that possibility from every angle," Craig reminded her. "We haven't found any evidence to corroborate that."

Hawk slid the picture back onto the corner of the desk. "Then let's get down to the specifics of the investigation to this point."

"If that's what you want." Craig looked to Alonsa instead of Hawk, as if he were giving her one last chance to back away from hiring him.

She didn't budge or waver.

Craig shrugged and went back to the seat behind his desk. He pulled another folder from the stack and started talking. An hour of discussion and note-taking later, it became clear that Craig had told them everything of value that he was going to share with them. Hawk was certain the information barely skirted what Craig had available to him.

Alonsa excused herself to go to the ladies' room. The tension in the room climbed to new levels as Craig leaned forward and propped his elbows on the desktop.

"I don't know how you talked Alonsa into hiring you," he said, "but if you're halfway honest you'll admit to her right now that you're not up to the job."

"And just why would I do that?"

"Because you have no idea what you're up against. Whatever experiences you've had as a commando aren't going to translate to this type of crime."

"That's a matter of opinion."

"It's fact. You're untrained when it comes to the abduction of a child. You're giving Alonsa false hope. Worse, you're putting her at risk."

"How do you figure that?"

"Todd was responsible for putting some very dangerous criminals in prison. You mess with these bastards and they won't just roll over and play dead because you're a big, tough navy SEAL."

"A former SEAL, and I thought you were convinced this wasn't connected to Todd."

"I am, but you start questioning these guys and you'll bring Alonsa to their attention all over again. There are guys in Texas who'd take her out for the price of a good steak."

"There are guys in every state who'll do that," Hawk said, "New York included."

"Right. So don't give them a reason."

"Did you back away from the investigation to protect Alonsa?"

Craig smirked as if the question were preposterous. "Of course not. I was in a position to protect her and I know what I'm dealing with."

He scooted his chair back from the desk and rubbed his chin. "I'm sure you're aware that even if you were to discover what happened to Lucy, Alonsa may not end up falling into your arms in gratitude. There's no guarantee this has a happy ending."

"I haven't promised one."

"All the same, Alonsa clings to the hope that her daughter's alive. Finding out differently could destroy her."

"I suspect she's stronger than you think," Hawk said.

"But you can't be sure of that."

"Nope, but I figure a mother deserves to know if her child is dead or alive. And if Lucy is alive, that's all the more reason that someone needs to find the truth of what happened to her. The FBI hasn't proven up to that task, so I figure I may as well give it a shot."

"If you let Alonsa get hurt, I'll hold you personally responsible."

Hawk stood. "She won't get hurt on my watch."

Craig walked over to stand in front of Hawk. "Your macho SEAL act doesn't impress me. I know what you're up to, and using a missing kid to get a roll between the sheets is about as low-down as you can get."

Hawk's muscles clenched and his fists knotted. He'd love to plant one of them in Craig's face, but starting a fight in an FBI facility didn't seem the best of ideas. Still, he stood toe to toe with the guy.

"I don't appreciate your suggestion that Alonsa can be seduced by an offer of help. And I don't manipulate women for sexual favors. I do finish what I start, so if you come across anything that will help me find Lucy, I'm always ready to hear it. Otherwise, stay out of my way."

If Alonsa noticed the tension between the two men when she entered the room, she made no mention of it. The meeting came to an abrupt end. Hawk and Alonsa left with a duplicate of the recently acquired photo, scrawled notes and copies of the limited information from the files that Craig deemed appropriate for them to have.

They hit the clogged streets of New York and entered the realm of blaring horns, exhaust fumes and layers of threatening clouds topping the skyscrapers.

A car skidded to a stop as the light at the corner turned red. "So exactly what is it you miss about New York?" Hawk teased. "The noise, the pollution or the lunatics behind the wheels?"

"Give it a chance," she said. "You just might grow to like it."

"Not unless they put in a pasture at every corner and pipe in a lot more sunlight than is getting past those sky-scrapers and clouds now."

"Let's get back to the hotel," she said. "We'll go to your room and go over the information from Craig."

His hotel room. A room dominated by a king-size bed while they pored over any and every aspect of Alonsa's late husband's life that could have had an effect on Lucy's abduction. Alonsa would be reminded again and again of the type of madman into whose hands her daughter might have been delivered.

She'd be vulnerable. He'd have to comfort her. And he'd be sucked into an avalanche of temptation that neither of them needed at the moment.

"How about we go to a coffee shop instead?" he suggested.

"Perfect. I could use an espresso."

That he could handle.

IT WAS THREE HOURS and pages of convoluted facts later when Hawk made it back to his hotel room for a shower. He went straight for the bathroom, turned on the hot water and kicked out of his shoes and socks. The temperature of the tile sent a jolt through his bloodstream. Six months out of the service and he was already growing soft.

Six months out and he was still trying to find himself. It had to be the same for Alonsa. No doubt she missed the life she'd had in New York, probably ached for the husband who'd been taken from her too soon, endured constant heartbreak for a daughter who she couldn't even be certain was still alive.

He missed being part of a team that worked as one when they were on a mission. Missed jumping from planes into total blackness trusting he'd be picked up from choppy waters in the black of night. Missed tramping through enemy-held territory with a backpack whose weight seemed to equal that of a small elephant.

Go figure.

He undressed and stepped beneath the pulsating

spray. He stood there for long minutes letting the water massage the muscles in his shoulders before pouring half the small bottle of shampoo into his hair and lathering.

He was just starting to relax when the truth sank into his brain. Dalliers had thought he was joining the game just to work his way into Alonsa's bed. He wasn't, but his reason might be even more selfish.

It was more than possible that he'd jumped into this because he craved real action.

You're putting Alonsa in danger.

Dalliers's words echoed through his mind.

Too late for second thoughts now. Alonsa was counting on him to do what he'd promised. If Lucy was alive, he'd find her. If not, he'd find out who was behind the kidnapping.

He'd keep Alonsa safe while he was doing it, but if he found out that someone had killed that little girl, heaven help them.

Dalliers might have the strength of the FBI behind him, but he also had their restrictions. Hawk made his own rules.

ALONSA HADN'T INTENDED to nap, but two restless nights had left her exhausted. Her eyes had closed almost the minute she'd stretched out across the bed and rested her head atop the soft pillow.

She'd waked just in time to shower and dress for dinner. They'd planned to dine at a quaint restaurant that had been in the area for years, only now the slush the weatherman had predicted had arrived.

Not quite snow, not quite sleet, not quite rain. She'd forgotten how it could set in like this in New York, leaving the city gray and frigid. The restaurant was several blocks away and available cabs would be slim, though she supposed the hotel could get one for them.

Picking up the remote, she flicked on the TV to catch the evening news. The lead story was the economy woes. The bright spot was the fact that the Giants were now favored in the upcoming playoff game.

There was a tap at the door. Hawk was early. She was about to turn off the TV when she heard a mention of a missing child. She froze to the spot. The anchor's next words sent the frigid paralysis clear down to the bone.

Chapter Five

Hawk knocked for the third time, louder this time. He knew Alonsa was in the room. He could hear the TV in the background. Finally, she unlatched the door and opened it a crack. Her eyes looked as haunted as they had the other night when she'd gotten the cruel phone call. Her face was ghostly white.

He pushed through the door and curled his hands around her forearms. "What's wrong?"

"They found a body of a little girl."

He swallowed the curses that flew to his mouth. Did she fall apart like this every time a child went missing? That had happened far too often of late.

"Here in New York?" he asked.

"In Houston. She was buried in a shallow grave in the backyard of a house in the Museum District. They think she may have been dead for up to four years."

Son of a bitch. No wonder this had hit so hard. Apprehension swept through him, though he struggled not to let Alonsa see it. "How did you hear this? Did someone call you?"

"No. I was watching a cable news channel."

"Was there any other information?"

"They estimate that she was between three and six years old when she died. The house's new owner unearthed the body when he took out an old greenhouse and dug up the ground to put in a garden."

Alonsa started to shake. Hawk pulled her into his arms. "I know this is frightening, but don't jump to conclusions, Alonsa. I'll call Cutter and see what he can learn from local sources. He has a good friend—someone called Goose—who's a detective with HPD. He should be able to give us specifics."

He led her to the chair next to the window with its spray of freezing rain tattooed across the pane. Cutter's cell phone was the best way to reach him, even if he was at the ranch. Hawk punched in the number.

While the call went through, he opened the minibar and pulled out a bottle of wine. The top was a screw-off. He opened it, poured half the contents into a glass and handed it to Alonsa.

She shook her head. "No thanks."

"It's medicinal." He set it on the table beside her as Cutter answered.

Hawk didn't bother with a customary greeting. "Did you catch the news tonight?"

"The child's body they found in Houston?"

"So you heard."

"Actually Linney heard it on the news a half hour ago. She called me and I contacted Goose Milburn immediately. He just got back to me with the little they've been able to put together. I was about to call you."

"Where do we stand?"

"The body hasn't been identified as yet, but Lucy

Salatoya has already been mentioned by reporters as a possibility. She was fodder for the local news media for months after her disappearance, so the connection was inevitable.

"The location where they found the body is within a few miles of the zoo. The rough estimate of the age of victim matches. So does the ballpark time since the body was buried."

"Damn." Hawk ran the scenario through his troubled mind. Not good. "But nothing concrete as yet?"

"No," Cutter assured him. "Houston has a population of millions. There could be any number of stories behind the grave. Anything can happen in a major metropolis these days."

Or in a small town for that matter. None of that would offer Alonsa the least bit of reassurance.

"Has Alonsa heard?" Cutter asked.

"Yeah. A few minutes ago."

"How's she taking it?"

"About as you'd expect."

"I didn't even consider the news going national so soon, or I'd have given you a heads-up even before I contacted Goose. Are you with her now?"

"I am." And would be until they got some kind of definitive word. There was no way he'd leave her alone with this hanging over her.

"Weird timing," Cutter said. "I mean just when you decide to take up the case, something like this explodes all over the news."

"Call me the second you hear something," Hawk said, ready to get off the phone and turn his attention back to Alonsa.

"I will. And you can call Goose yourself if you like. I filled him in on your connection with the case."

"Thanks."

Once he'd written down the number, he muttered a quick goodbye and broke the connection. The wine he'd poured for Alonsa was untouched and she was biting a well-manicured nail. She looked up to him for encouragement that he couldn't give.

He walked over and sat on the arm of her chair. "There's still no identification of the body."

"They have Lucy's picture on file. Can't they at least see if it looks like her?"

"Give them time." He slipped an arm around her shoulders. The answer to her question would be obvious once she thought about it, but he didn't want to bring up how the body would have decayed over two years in a shallow grave.

"Was that Cutter you were talking to?"

"It was. Linney heard the news and alerted him. He's talked to his buddy with the Houston Police Department and they've promised to keep him in the loop."

"I want to know everything he told you."

Hawk filled her in, giving it to her straight.

"I want to talk to the HPD," she said when he finished. "They worked with me on the original abduction. They should be willing to talk to me now."

He nodded. "I'll get Goose on the line for you."

Goose didn't answer. She made the next call herself, finally connecting with a desk sergeant. Hawk knew from her grim expression that there was no change in the news.

When she broke the connection, she stood and stared

out the window at the bank of neighboring skyscrapers. Their lights had turned on, casting rectangular halos of illumination through the mist.

He hated moments like this, never knew what he should do or if he should do anything at all. Most of his male military buddies tended to pull away when they were worried, shrink into themselves and escape to thoughts that lay buried in the recesses of their brains.

That had worked well for Hawk. He'd perfected the emotional denial method years before he reached manhood.

Alonsa likely needed more. He stepped behind her and put a hand on her shoulder. Her muscles were tight. Her fear was palpable, like a suffocating force that sucked the oxygen from the room. He felt it as poignantly as if it were his own.

"He couldn't tell me anything," she said, "except what we already know."

She turned away from the window, walked back to the bedside table and pulled their reservations from her handbag. "I'm going to call and see if we can get a flight out tonight."

And then what? he wondered. Would she insist on going into Houston and seeing what had to be the frightful remains of the body that she had no real evidence was her daughter? He could think of little worse.

"It will be difficult to get to the airport in this weather."

"I don't care how difficult it is. I just want to go home. I need to be there."

"Then let me make the call for you."

She nodded and sat on the side of the bed while he made the call. He did try, but there were no direct flights back to Houston that night and the only indirect route that could get them there before morning was fully booked. Like it or not, she was stuck in New York until morning.

She took the explanation better than he'd expected. No tears or outrage, just continued anxiety that seemed to shake her to her core. It was going to be a long night. Sitting and waiting and staring at the rain would be agony for both of them.

"You'll need to eat something," he said. "Do you want to go out or would you rather order something from room service?"

"I couldn't eat. Just order for yourself."

He skimmed the room service menu. He wasn't hungry either, and that might be a first for him. But this was a different kind of edginess than he was used to. Nothing about tonight was within his control.

Still, they needed food. He ordered ham sandwiches, bowls of chicken tortilla soup, a bottle of better cabernet than was offered in the in-room bar and a selection of fruits and cheeses. Perhaps if it was there, Alonsa would munch on something.

She slipped out of her shoes and pulled her stockinged feet to the bed, pushing the pillows against the headboard and leaning against them.

"It's always like this," she said. "I convince myself that Lucy is alive. I'm her mother. I should know if she weren't. I should feel it deep inside me. But then they find a body and my heart feels as if it's being ripped from my chest."

"So this isn't the first time for this?"

"No. It's happened twice before. The first time was only a few months after Lucy had disappeared. A young girl's body was discovered in a Texas border town. Apparently the victim fit Lucy's description. One of the reporters who'd covered the original abduction called and wanted a statement from me."

"Hard to believe anyone could be that insensitive."

"She probably figured if she didn't get to me, someone else would."

"You're much too forgiving."

"Carrying a grudge takes too much energy."

Yet carrying a grudge was what some criminals did best. Craig had made a point of telling him that today. Their grudges would be against Todd Salatoya, but Alonsa would pay if they exacted revenge.

Craig didn't believe the kidnapping was payback, but Craig was human and humans made mistakes.

Alonsa's cell phone jangled. She grabbed it, then stared at it without answering. "It's Craig. I'm sure he's heard and wants to offer me a fake reassurance."

"Do you want me to take the call for you?"

"No. Just let it ring. I'll call him back later."

There was a tapping at the door and Hawk opened it for the food delivery. The guy rolled in the cart laden with food, silverware and a vase with three pink roses. The waiter smiled affably, no doubt believing that they were having a romantic rendezvous.

Hawk tipped the guy. Before he was out the door, Hawk's cell phone rang. Probably Craig trying to reach Alonsa through him since she hadn't answered. He yanked the phone from his pocket.

The caller ID said out of area. "Hawk Taylor," he said, taking the call.

"Goose Milburn here. I'm a buddy of Cutter's. He said you're with Alonsa Salatoya in New York tonight."

"I am."

"I have news."

Hawk's chest tightened. Alonsa stood and pushed close to him. He mouthed the word *Goose* and pulled her into the circle of his arm.

"Good news," Goose said, "at least for Alonsa. The body they found today is not her daughter."

Relief swept through him in waves. "Are you sure?"

"Positive. The girl was an—"

"Wait," Hawk said. "Alonsa should hear this for herself." He pushed the phone into her hands. "Great news," he whispered.

He held her close as her eyes brimmed with tears of thanksgiving and her words became whispered mutterings. She'd been given a respite.

But for how long? And would he be the one responsible one day for delivering the dreaded news from which there would never be a respite?

No matter. He'd made a commitment. He'd accepted the mission. Giving up was not an option.

ALONSA'S MUSCLES condensed to liquid, her breath to vapor. She'd been held together by fear and dread and when they'd evaporated, she simply folded in on herself.

Goose's words drifted in the semi-fog of her mind, only half registering—all except the beautiful truth that the body was not Lucy.

Then just as quickly, her energy spiked and her mood lifted until she felt she were floating on the very air that had suffocated her moments before.

"Thank you." She tried to think of the man's name on the other end of the line. She couldn't, but it didn't matter. "Thank you so much."

"No problem."

"Have you identified the victim?"

He filled her in with the basics. When he finished she thanked him again.

"Okay, you have a good evening. Make Hawk take you out for a drink."

"Just breathing is enough right now."

"I understand. You take care, and if there's ever anything I can do to help, let me know."

"Believe me, I will. You're a lifesaver."

"Always glad to deliver news like this."

Tears were streaming down her face as she broke the connection and turned back to Hawk. He pulled a tissue from the box at her elbow and wiped the excess water from her cheeks and the corners of her eyes.

Her vision was blurred by the salty dampness but it was as if she were seeing Hawk for the very first time. All the charm from the other night was still there. The thick, dark hair, the classic nose, piercing eyes the color of chocolate creams. And muscles. What muscles! He was the poster boy of rugged virility with a hunk factor that topped the charts.

And none of that began to describe the appeal of this stranger who'd walked into her life and handed her back the will to fight to find Lucy all over again.

He was the man who'd find Lucy. The certainty of

that hit her with mesmerizing force. That's why she'd gone to the party at Linney's that she hadn't planned to attend. That's why Brandon had fallen and hit his head. This was meant to be.

She slipped into Hawk's arms again and he held her close. The realization of how well she fit barely grazed her mind as the newfound optimism bubbled inside her like a flute of expensive champagne.

When she pulled away, she spied the food, or at least the part that was uncovered. Huge hunks of brown bread. A mix of exotic cheeses. Luscious berries peeking from beneath a mound of Chantilly cream. Suddenly she was famished. She chose a square of white creamy cheese and popped it into her mouth.

Hawk propped his backside against the desk and smiled at her. "What a difference a phone call can make."

"That one sure did. And even better, the little girl whose body they found hadn't been murdered, at least not if their facts are right."

"What are the facts?"

"I'll fill you in while we eat."

He removed the metal warming lids with a flourish and dragged the striped club chair up to the cart, standing behind it and holding it in place until she settled into it.

"Who knew that navy SEALs had such manners?"

"Only when in plush hotel rooms. In the heat of battle we're total slobs. Come to think of it, I'm not sure I've ever been in a hotel room quite this plush. An old haunt of yours?"

"No. I paid for it with points. It emptied my cache."

Hawk lifted the bottle of wine and filled both their glasses. This time she took a sip. "Nice," she said.

"Luck of the draw. I'm generally a beer man."

"I'll keep that in mind." She spooned a bit of the soup into her mouth and savored the spicy warmth as it slid down her throat. Minutes ago she'd been drowning in dreaded possibilities. Now the relief was so rich, she felt as if she were in New York on vacation. And for hotel food, this wasn't half-bad.

She related the details from her conversation with Goose. They believed the body to be that of a young girl who'd died in the house five years ago from complications due to the flu. Neighbors recalled that the family living in the back apartment of the house had said the five-year-old had been taken back to Mexico for burial.

The HPD had tracked down a member of the family and he'd admitted that they'd buried her in the backyard because they had no money for a funeral. They'd been afraid to ask for financial assistance because at the time they were in the country illegally. Now they were citizens and living in Livingston, Texas. The child's remains would finally be buried properly.

"Too bad they didn't find that out before the shark reporters got wind of it," Hawk said.

"But I have this really good feeling about things now," Alonsa admitted. "You're going to find Lucy, Hawk. I have this incredible premonition that you will."

"It's not incredible," Hawk assured her. "I fully intend to find out who abducted her and why. That's all I can promise."

From most men even that kind of promise would have seemed arrogant. Coming from Hawk, it seemed natural and reassuring. He didn't just talk the talk, he'd walked the walk for years in Special Ops. He had reason to be sure of himself, and that was good enough for Alonsa.

By the time they'd finished eating, the sleet had changed to snow. The delicate flakes drifted in the wind and had begun to mound on the window ledge. Snow was another thing she'd missed about living in New York.

Not that she liked the muddy slush it left behind when it melted or the black smudged mounds that stayed for days on the sides of the street. But when the snow was falling, Manhattan transformed into a mystical fairyland.

Lucy had been only two when she'd taken her for her first sledding adventure in Central Park. Alonsa had bundled her up in a blue snowsuit and a pair of psychedelic boots that made her look like a twirling ball as they'd flown down the hill together.

Lucy's high-pitched laughter echoed through her mind now. She shifted and curled around the sound, growing antsy now that her hunger was abated.

"Let's go for a walk," she said. "We'll save the fruit and cheese until we come back and have it with the rest of the wine."

"A capital idea." Hawk finished the remainder of his sandwich in a less than dainty bite. She put the cheese and fruit on the bedside table and hurried to get into her black wool coat and her red hat, scarf and gloves. She didn't remember Craig's call until they were walking out the door. She'd get back to him later.

Odd how quickly she'd shifted her reliance from

him to Hawk Taylor. Hawk opened the door and they stepped into the hall together. His hand rested on the small of her back. His shoulder brushed hers.

A vibrating spark hopped along her nerve endings. She took a deep breath in hopes of extinguishing the titillating awareness. This was only a walk in the snow.

A LOOSE BOARD SQUEAKED beneath the woman's bare feet as she padded away from the back door and toward the flowering shrubs that bordered the deck of her new home, the night's excitement still coursing her veins.

The mystery hadn't lasted nearly long enough, but the reporter had brought up the fact that the daughter of Todd and Alonsa Salatoya had gone missing near that same spot two years ago.

Surely Alonsa had heard. She would have been devastated at the morbid discovery of the small child's grave.

That thought stuck in the woman's mind and she smiled as she pulled her sweater tight over her breasts before taking one last look at the stars and going back inside the dark, quiet house.

Chapter Six

Hawk jerked awake with the first bang of trash cans on the street ten floors below him. The dinginess of a cloudy dawn peeked through the window, outlining the zigzagged mound of snow on the ledge.

An uneasy sort of need crackled inside him. He hadn't been that fond of snow before last night. Now he'd never watch flakes fall from the sky without thinking of Alonsa.

He'd had plenty of other women in his life, though he wasn't nearly the ladies' man the other frogmen made him out to be. Women just seemed to like him and he appreciated the finer qualities of the opposite sex.

He got the physical connection. It was simple and natural.

What had happened last night with Alonsa went miles beyond that. Seeing her so distraught, reacting to her agonizing heartbreak, realizing how fragile and yet how strong she was at the same time. It had made him feel things deep inside where he didn't like to feel at all. Where he hadn't even known he could feel.

And then they'd walked and talked in the snow. Nothing spectacular, just conversation but the feelings inside didn't let up. Sure he wanted her physically. That was a given. What man wouldn't?

It was all the other sensations stirring inside him that made him nervous. Like the need to wrap her up inside him so he could absorb all her hurt.

Damn. He sounded like a schoolboy with his first crush. He slung his legs over the side of the bed, stretching as the balls of his feet hit the thick carpeted floor. The stack of files and notes he'd gotten from Craig glared reproachfully at him as he walked past them to take care of business in the bathroom.

The files and the search for Alonsa's daughter was where his focus should be, not on emotional complexities he couldn't even pretend to comprehend.

The worst of it all was that Craig had been right about his areas of expertise not including child abductions or missing persons investigations. On the other hand, he had incredible instincts and an uncanny ability to see through the camouflage of the most cunning adversaries. Not hyperbole. Just the facts.

He washed his hands, splashed his face with water and ordered a pot of black coffee from room service. By the time the brew arrived, he'd settled in on a plan of operation, or at least the beginning of one.

By the time dawn became a golden glow, he knew exactly where he planned to start.

ALONSA STUFFED HER boots with dirty clothes and shoved them into the shoe pocket of her carry-on. She wasn't due to meet Hawk for the cab ride to the airport for another two hours, but she was dressed and ready to go.

Her mood was far lighter going home than it had

been when they were leaving Dobbin. She'd even found herself dancing to a catchy commercial tune on TV as she'd dressed.

The change could partly stem from the relief she'd felt last night after hearing that the recovered body wasn't her daughter. But it was also the newfound hope of finding Lucy. Hawk would charge forward with his investigation even though Craig had tried to discourage him and make him doubt his ability.

Even the return to New York hadn't been the emotional disaster she'd feared. Hawk was probably at least partly to credit for that, as well. He hadn't pushed for conversation on their walk last night, hadn't asked about Todd or the life they'd shared here. Hadn't even questioned her about her career.

He'd just been there, flashing that boyish smile of his and making comments about the people and the weather that made her laugh.

She opened the drawers in the bathroom to be sure she hadn't left anything unpacked, then checked her reflection in the mirror one last time. Good to go, she decided, with plenty of time remaining for a quick breakfast in the hotel coffee shop.

The phone in the hotel room jangled. She hurried to answer it. "Hello."

"Good morning." The deep timbre of Hawk's voice rang in her ear.

"I was just heading down to the lobby for a bagel and coffee," she said. "Care to join me?"

"Not for a bagel, but breakfast sounds good. Also wanted to let you know that I called and changed my flight plans for today."

"Why would you do that?"

"There's this woman in Jackson, Mississippi."

"A woman?" She swallowed a rush of irritation that hit from out of the blue. "Fine."

"Not what you're thinking," he added quickly.

She had no idea how he'd know what she was thinking when she didn't know herself.

"I've been up since before dawn," he continued, "looking over the information Craig provided. Since I'm coming into this so many months after the fact, I decided it makes sense for me to retrace the steps of the original investigation from the beginning."

"You've already visited the spot of the abduction."

"I know. Now I'm concentrating on the early possible sightings of Lucy, especially those which reported that she was traveling with a female. One of those was called in by a woman named Marilyn Couric who was visiting Jackson, Mississippi, at the time. She lives there now."

"I'm not sure it's worth the stop. There have been dozens of reported sightings over the years. All were investigated. None led anywhere."

"I think this one is worth checking out again."

"Why?"

"The timing for one thing. If the kidnapper drove straight through from Houston to Jackson, occasionally exceeding the speed limit and not stopping for any lengthy period of time, she could have made it in under six hours."

"Anything else?"

"The woman's profession."

"What kind of work does she do?"

"Portrait painting. I figure she'd be good with faces,

recognize the shape and the lines, the angles and indiscriminate features someone else might overlook. And she says she saw Lucy's picture on TV just a few moments before she spotted a girl who looked exactly like her in a service station."

"And we know Lucy left the zoo with a woman." Did she dare hope this could turn into a real lead? "I want to go with you," she said, making an instant decision.

Her request was met with silence. She didn't see why it should be a problem. "If you've changed your flight, we can change mine as well."

"This is just a place to start, Alonsa. Don't go expecting instant miracles."

But if the woman in Jackson could give them a description of the abductor, this would be as close to a miracle as they'd had. "I'm going with you," she repeated, her tone leaving no doubt she meant business.

Craig had stressed throughout the investigation that he was the expert and she was just the grieving mother. She wasn't going to go that route again. "I'd like to be in on the questioning."

"What about Brandon?" Hawk asked.

Brandon. Cripes. She couldn't just expect Linney to keep him all day without checking with her first. "I'll give Linney a call and get back to you."

"Whatever you decide, meet me in the coffee shop downstairs. I'll be the one with all the artery-clogging fats and carbs spilling off the plate."

"Right." Carbs that hardened into six-pack abs. She broke the connection and punched in Linney's home number. She wouldn't expect miracles, but she wouldn't turn one down, either. She was past due.

LINNEY TURNED TO HER gorgeous hunk of a husband who was stretched out on the bed next to her. He reached for her, cupped her right breast in his hand and massaged her erect nipple with his thumb.

It was part of their morning routine of kissing, touching and savoring of their naked bodies which almost always led to making love. This morning's routine had been interrupted by a phone call from Alonsa Salatoya.

"Trouble in the Big Apple?" Cutter asked.

"To the contrary. It must be going well. Alonsa wants me to watch Brandon until early evening so that they can take a later flight back to Houston."

Cutter slid closer and kissed the tip of her nose. "Yet you sound worried."

"I just hate to see her pin too much hope on Hawk. I don't want her to get hurt. She's been through so much."

"Aren't you the one who threw the matchmaking into gear almost the minute you met Hawk?"

"I am," she admitted reluctantly. "But it never dawned on me that he'd take on a new search for her missing daughter. I thought you had work for him to do."

"The project he's going to head for me isn't ready to start yet. He's got time to get his feet wet in the search for Lucy Salatoya."

"The search has been going on for two years. If the FBI hasn't been able to find out what happened to Lucy, I can't see how Hawk Taylor is just going to swoop down and sniff out new clues."

"That's because you don't know Hawk the way I do. I have complete confidence that he'll ferret out all the facts."

"And if he finds out Lucy was murdered or worse, horribly tortured and sexually abused first, Alonsa may never be able to climb out of the despair. She barely survived the abduction as it was."

"You didn't even know her then," he reminded her.

"No, but I've heard all about it from Merlee. That little girl was Alonsa's life and to lose her right after her husband had been shot and killed all but destroyed her. Knowing Brandon needed his mother was the only thing that kept her going. I just can't bear to think of her going through that again."

Cutter pulled her into his arms. "Don't you think you're overreacting a bit to a phone call from a woman who was feeling good about this situation?"

Probably. Her hormones had been a wreck the last few days. It wasn't like her at all. "I want Hawk to find Lucy. I do, but only if there's a happy ending."

Cutter didn't offer any words of reassurance to that. He never lied to her. That was another of the things she loved about him.

"So exactly what did Alonsa have to say?" Cutter asked.

Linney filled him in on the developments and their scheduled stop in Jackson. He agreed with Hawk and Alonsa that it was a wise move.

"Are you sure you're up to keeping Brandon another day?" he asked. "I've got some business that can't wait but I can ask Aunt Merlee to cancel her plan to visit her friend Josie this afternoon."

"Absolutely not. I love having Brandon here. He's

so curious and fun and adorable. Which reminds me. He'll be waking any minute now and wanting his breakfast." She rolled away from Cutter to get out of bed.

"But he's not up yet." Cutter caught her around the waist and tugged her back down beside him.

His lips found hers and his hand roamed her abdomen.

"You're insatiable, Mr. Martin."

"Comes from sleeping with a gorgeous, naked woman, Mrs. Martin."

And then he showed her just how marvelously insatiable he was.

HAWK FOLLOWED ALONSA into Marilyn Couric's studio, which was on the top floor of a historic building in the Arts Fondren District. The studio consisted of bare brick walls, a high ceiling and a large open space lined on the east by a row of six foot high, uncovered windows.

Around the space were rectangular, paint-splattered tables and easels and numerous uncluttered shelves containing baskets of supplies. A cozy nook occupied one corner, apparently for preparing and eating quick meals and relaxing or discussing projects with her clients.

Not only did the space contain all the fixtures of a consummate artist, Marilyn was dressed the role as well. The pencil-thin woman wore a loose smock splattered with so many colors it looked like a mad painter's work of modern art.

Her brown hair was braided. Her slightly wrinkled skin was ruddy, as if it had just been scrubbed with a coarse cloth. Her smile was engaging. She looked to be anywhere from forty to fifty, maybe older.

She slipped out of the smock and dropped it onto a scarred wooden barstool near a blank canvas as she led them to a worn sofa near the microwave and small retro metal kitchen table. "Excuse my appearance," she said, brushing the wrinkles from her pink loose-fitting blouse.

"My two o'clock appointment didn't show up so I was busy putting the finishing touches on a painting of one of our local fireman who was killed in the line of duty. I like to do that for the families of fallen heroes when I can. You know, giving back and all that."

"It sounds like a very charitable thing to do," Alonsa said.

Hawk couldn't help but compare the gait of the two women walking in front of him. Marilyn was all business, her flat-heeled Birkenstocks slapping the hard floor, her arms swinging nonchalantly at her side, braids bobbing.

There was nothing wrong with her walk. It just lacked the tantalizing rhythm or grace that Alonsa exhibited with seemingly no effort.

An unwanted urge hardened somewhere near his groin. He shook his head as if that would clear the disturbing sensation. It didn't.

"Can I get you something to drink?" the artist asked. "I have chilled wine or a hot herbal tea." She opened a dorm-size refrigerator. "Or bottled water if you prefer."

"The tea sounds delightful," Alonsa said.

"My favorite refresher," Marilyn said. "I'll join you."

Hawk opted for water. He sat next to Alonsa on the sofa. Marilyn served the drinks then settled on one of the two straight-backed, mismatched chairs that she'd pulled away from the table.

"I was really surprised to get your call this

morning," Marilyn said. Her attention turned to Alonsa. "I didn't realize your daughter was still missing. It's been what, a year?"

"Two."

"I'm so sorry. This must be devastating for you."

"It is. That's why I really hope you can help us."

"I don't see how I can. I told the police all I know, not that they seemed that interested. I think they doubted the veracity of my report."

"I can't explain that," Alonsa admitted, "but some new information's come to light recently. We have reason to believe that the abductor was a woman."

Marilyn nodded. "That agrees with what I saw, but still I don't know how I can help."

Hawk rubbed his jawline with a crooked thumb. "Did you get a good look at the woman?"

"Not as good as I would have liked. It all happened so fast."

"According to the report you gave the police, the girl was in the backseat of the car when you spotted her," Hawk said. "How is it that you got such a good look at her?"

"Now you sound like the police," Marilyn said. "They expressed the same doubts, but I was parked at the opposite pump and I can assure you that I saw the child's face distinctly. She had it pressed to the glass. Her eyes had a blank expression, as if she'd been drugged."

Hawk heard the quick intake of Alonsa's breath as she hugged her arms tightly around her chest.

"Was she hurt?" Alonsa asked quickly. "Were there bruises?"

"Not that I could see. She wasn't crying. She just looked out of it. I should have yelled or jumped inside the car or even attacked the woman, but I just didn't think that fast."

"I don't understand," Alonsa said. "What happened?"

"The woman was pumping gas but when she noticed me so near her back door, she jumped back in her car and took off. She left the nozzle dangling."

"Can you give us even a vague description of the woman?" Hawk asked.

"I doubt I could pick her out in a lineup, which is what the police asked me. Under the circumstances, I wouldn't trust my skills of observation to that degree. I did make a quick sketch of my impressions of her right after I called 911, though."

A sketch wasn't as good as a valid description but Hawk figured it beat nothing. "Did anyone from the FBI visit you to talk about the incident?"

"No, just a local policeman, and that was by phone. I offered him the sketch. He said he'd come by to pick it up, but I never saw him. Like I said, I don't think he was too impressed once he realized I didn't get a really good look at the abductor. He did promise to see that the investigation team got the report. I'm assuming they did or you wouldn't know to visit me now."

"Do you still have the sketch?" Hawk asked.

She nodded. "Would you like to see it?"

"Yes." Alonsa answered for him and the eagerness in her voice made him wince. He was still confident he could produce results, but not overnight. If she was going to live or die on every move he made, this would be incredibly hard on her.

"I'll be right back," Marilyn said. She walked to a tall, gray file cabinet near the shelving and returned with a manila folder. She took out a drawing and handed it to Alonsa.

Hawk shifted for a better view. The drawing was in pencil, the features loosely defined, but still detailed enough that if someone knew the woman they might have recognized her.

A laundry list of information bordered the right side of the sheet of plain white paper.

Hair: Reddish brown
Age: Mid-thirties
Body Build: Thin to average
Dress: Wrinkled denim capris and green T-shirt.

Hawk weighed each of the items in his mind, impressed by the specificities the artist had noted.

Alonsa's grip tightened, wrinkling the corner of the paper for a second before she pushed it toward Hawk. "It's not the same woman who left the zoo with Lucy. Her hair was blond and much longer. And she was dressed differently."

"I'm so very sorry if I've just made this harder on you," the artist said. Her eyes sought out Hawk's. "But I'm almost sure that was Lucy Salatoya I saw in that car. If not, the likeness was remarkable."

"We're not ruling out that possibility," Hawk said. "Do you mind if I keep the drawing?"

"By all means, keep it. I just wish I could have been more help."

He and Alonsa both expressed their thanks again.

Alonsa's voice remained reasonably steady. Her demeanor didn't. Brutal disappointment glazed her dark eyes and tugged at the corners of her lips. He felt the overpowering urge to take her in his arms and offer…

Offer what? Emotional support? He had to be crazy to even think he could do that. He was a machine. A laughing, loving, calculating, emotionless machine. His commanding officer had praised him for that. His ex-wife hadn't.

Still, when his arm brushed Alonsa's on the way to the rental car they'd picked up at the airport, the need to protect her from all this felt like chunks of solid metal rattling around inside him.

Alonsa buckled her seat belt, then picked up the drawing Hawk had propped against the canister between their seats. "Why bother with this sketch? It's obviously not the woman who kidnapped Lucy."

"Same body build," Hawk said. "That's really all we have to go on."

"Not the same hair." Frustration spiked her words. "Not wearing the same clothes."

"Hair and clothes are easy to change."

"Then you think this could actually be a sketch of the woman who has Lucy?"

"I never rule out anything until I know for certain it's impossible."

"So what do we do with the sketch?" She shifted, turning to face him.

"Find the woman in the sketch and check her out," he said. Easier said than done, but he wouldn't bring that up at the moment.

"I like the way you think, Hawk Taylor. I like it a

lot." A hint of a smile touched her lips as she reached across the seat and trailed the fingers of her right hand down his arm.

The casual touch sent unwanted urges crashing through him at the speed of a bullet. He was pretty sure she would not like what he was thinking now.

Then again, maybe she would.

BRANDON MET ALONSA at the front door of the house at the Double M with an eager hug and endless chatter about the horses. Apparently Linney had put him in the saddle with her and taken him for his first ride.

"Come see the horseys, Mommy. Come see them," he'd bubbled, until they'd all set out on a walk to the barn so that his mother could see the magnificent animal that had given him such a thrill.

Hawk and Cutter brought up the rear of the procession, dawdling and staying far enough behind the others so they could talk privately. Hawk filled Cutter in on the afternoon's meeting with Marilyn Couric.

"You should show the sketch to the HPD," Cutter said. "Maybe they can match it to someone's mug shot or one of the city's usual suspects."

"You'd think they would have done that before now. Hard to believe no one ever got back to Ms. Couric and requested the sketch."

"For some reason they must have ruled it out as a valid sighting."

"Yeah, and that was probably because they were convinced at the time the kidnapping was connected to the drug cartel that Todd had been trying to trap the night he got killed."

"But now you say the FBI thinks it was a random act."

"So says Craig Dalliers."

"What say you?" Cutter asked.

"I'd probably agree were it not for the phone calls that someone uses to torment Alonsa."

"But the calls don't really sound like the work of a drug cartel, either," Cutter offered.

"Not violent enough for a hardened criminal," Hawk agreed. "Too cruel and vindictive for someone who participated in a spur-of-the moment crime."

"Falls outside the box," Cutter said, "which is probably why the case is still unsolved."

"But not unsolvable," Hawk argued.

"Not with you on the job. So how are you and Alonsa hitting it off?"

"What makes you think there's any hitting going on?"

"The way you look at her. The way she looks at you."

"I look at her with my two eyes, same as I do anyone else."

"Tell that to someone who doesn't know you the way I do. Have you kissed her yet?"

"I'm not the kind to kiss and tell."

"You haven't, have you?" Cutter gave him a knowing grin. "But you gotta be thinking about it. Good-looking woman like Alonsa and the two of you spending so much time together. Yep. You gotta be working up to the first kiss. Can't believe you haven't made the move on her yet."

"Haven't and don't plan to. I may not be getting paid, but this is still a job. The stakes are too high to invite unnecessary complications."

"You're a smart man, but I knew that when I signed you on."

Carne ran back to check on them, decided they were not as interesting as the party he'd left and went back to yap a few times and run circles around Brandon and the women.

Linney turned and propped her hands on her shapely hips. "Are you two coming with us or what?"

"We're coming," Cutter said, picking up his pace.

Hawk picked his up as well, only now his thoughts were all about Alonsa's full lips and what they'd feel like crushed beneath his. The thought became a slow burn that burrowed deep inside him.

No, he told himself, being with Alonsa was all about business and wasn't likely to ever be anything more, not even when the case was solved. A sophisticated, big-city widow with kids. A cowboy type who'd never been able to fill the emotional needs of anyone.

And yet there were those lips… He and Cutter had caught up with the women now and he saw Alonsa smiling up at him, her lips so tempting he could all but taste them.

How much could a normal, red-blooded man take without giving in?

Chapter Seven

Goose Milburn was off duty the following day and so eager to take a look at the sketch drawn by Marilyn Couric that he made the hour-plus drive to Dobbin. When Hawk arrived at Alonsa's, Goose's unmarked Ford was already parked in her driveway. He heard Goose's booming voice even before he reached the door. He rang the bell and waited.

Alonsa flung the door open. "Did you bring the sketch?"

He removed his black Stetson and raked his fingers through his hair. "That's why you invited me to the party, isn't it?"

"You're always invited to the party."

He wasn't quite sure how to take that, but decided now was not the time to give it much thought. Not with her looking like a model in a pair of black trousers and a white silky blouse that draped her perky breasts to perfection.

Her lips were a glossy red. A pair of silver earrings danced about her high cheekbones when she moved her head to nod him inside.

Brandon ran in and wrapped his short arms around Alonsa's hips while he stared up at Hawk. "Now we gots two companys."

"Mommy's got company, sweetheart. You can go play. Goose is in the kitchen," she said to Hawk. "Come on back."

Brandon was not to be ignored that easily. He scooted over to Hawk's side. "Wanna watch me ride my tractor?"

"Later," Alonsa said, answering for Hawk. "We have some business to talk about. You can play in the backyard, though."

"Yippee!" And he was off. Carne showed up just in time to skid into a turn and follow him.

Hawk followed Alonsa to the kitchen. Goose was sitting at the table, nursing a cup of coffee. He got up and they went through the introductions.

"So you're Cutter's latest recruit," Goose said. "I tried to get him to go to work for the HPD, but he hates rules and bureaucracy."

"Can you blame him?"

"Goes with living in a civilized world. You get used to them. But Cutter's got the ideal life going for him out here in Dobbin. Ranching and investigating, not necessarily in that order. Not to mention a beautiful wife."

They exchanged the customary pleasantries while Hawk helped himself to a cup of coffee. They'd talked on the phone last night so Goose already knew the story behind the sketch. Hawk set his mug on the table and pulled the drawing from a black notebook filled with his notes on the abduction case.

Goose studied it for moment then held it up to get the benefit of the sun's light pouring though the back window. He shook his head after a brief inspection and let the sketch slide from his fingers back to the table.

"Nothing here that strikes me as familiar. There were dozens of calls from people who claimed to have seen Lucy in the first days after the abduction. Most of them were obviously mistaken. How much confidence do you have that the woman who made this sketch actually saw Lucy and the abductor?"

"Enough that I think you can list the woman in the sketch as a person of interest and spread the picture around in an effort to find her."

"Then you're talking better than fifty percent?"

"I'd say better than ninety percent." Hawk knew he didn't have any real grounds for making that assumption other than his gut feeling, but he'd depended on that to keep him alive when a wrong move could have sent his body parts flying in different directions. No need to doubt it now.

"Then consider it done," Goose said. "Cutter says you have the best instincts he's ever seen." Goose scooted his chair back from the table. "Can I take the sketch with me?"

"Sure," Hawk said. "I've made several copies."

"I'll check this out further, but don't pin too much hope on the results."

"And check for other suspects," Alonsa said. "We know now that it was a woman who kidnapped Lucy. That surely narrows the scope of the original investigation. You can rule out all the male registered sex offenders."

"Of which there are way too many roaming the streets," Hawk said. And unfortunately there were female perverts out there as well.

"Not a lot we can do about that. We arrest them. Judges and jails release them." Goose leaned back and sipped his coffee.

That pretty much concluded the encounter. A few crumbs gained. Not much more. Hawk grabbed his hat and walked with them to the door as Goose left.

There was no reason for him not to head to his truck, as well, except that Alonsa was standing so close he was drowning in the flowery fragrance of her.

So he kept standing in the same spot, wondering what it would be like to lower his mouth to hers and feel her hot breath mingling with his. With any other woman he wouldn't have hesitated.

But Alonsa wasn't just any woman. She was a client and much too vulnerable to be taken advantage of by a man with nothing to offer beyond immediate satisfaction.

"I'd invite you to stay for lunch," she said, "but I'm enrolling Brandon in the church preschool today." Her voice wavered a little on the word enrolling, but ended on a note of determination.

Hawk's thoughts switched gears, landing him back in blunt reality. "That's a big move for a woman who never lets her son out of her sight. What about those pesky field trips?"

"I'll sweat them out when the time comes. I know Brandon needs to be around other children and the program is more a play opportunity for three-year-olds than anything else. I have to think of what's best for him."

"Way to go, Alonsa. Or is it break a leg, when you're talking to a performer?"

"A has-been performer," she corrected. "I've forgotten all the moves."

"Not all of them."

She stepped closer and looked up at him, her eyes hinting at a spark that needed to be kindled. Her lips were parted seductively, inviting. A man would have to be crazy not to—

"Mom."

Brandon came running down the hall with Carne at his heels.

Saved by another man's kid and a yapping dog. "Guess that's my signal to ride off into the sunset," Hawk said.

"It's not even midday yet."

"It's five o'clock somewhere." He tipped his hat.

"To be continued," she whispered.

He pretended not to hear.

ALONSA STARTED THE CAR and drove away from the church only to stop at the end of the driveway, heart heavy and fighting tears. Every mother went through this. She'd heard their tales of the first time they'd walked away leaving their precious child with a teacher who saw them only as a member of the class.

Mothers and children had all survived the ordeal without any permanent scars. But those mothers hadn't already lost a child in one bizarre instant, let go of their hand never to hold it again.

Grabbing a tissue from her pocket, she dabbed the burning spillover from the corners of her eyes. She couldn't think that way. She would hold Lucy's hand again. She would. Hawk would see that she did. She only had to have faith.

And Brandon would be fine. He'd hardly noticed her leave, his attention too focused on the block area and the new and imaginative toys waiting there. She put the car in gear again and drove away slowly, the church disappearing from her rearview mirror.

She dreaded the thought of going back to her empty house. She could call Esteban and see if Keidra Shelton was ready for her to start on her house.

But that would mean she might not get back in time to pick up Brandon from his first day at preschool. She had no intention of turning that job over to anyone else.

She was five miles from her house, three from the Double M. She could stop off and have coffee with Linney.

Who was she kidding? She'd be there in hope of seeing Hawk. It had been almost three days since they'd met with Goose. Three days since Hawk's lips had been inches from hers and she'd been dizzy with the anticipation of his kiss.

They'd talked by phone a half-dozen times since then. They'd discussed Craig and the fact that he was not returning her calls to discuss why his investigative team had disregarded Marilyn Couric's sighting. Discussed the fact that Goose had had no luck with matching the sketch to a suspect. He hadn't mentioned their getting together.

Her cell phone jangled. Likely Craig with a multitude of excuses. "Hello."

"Is this the mother of preschool student Brandon Salatoya?"

Her heart skipped. "Hawk."

"I was thinking of you and wondering if you'd survived the big separation moment."

"I didn't cry and cling."

"Good for you."

"How did you know this was Brandon's first day?"

"Linney mentioned it when I stopped off at the main house to see Cutter. Are you busy this morning?"

"Just dreading going home to the empty nest."

"Would you mind if I stopped by?"

"Are there new developments?"

"Nothing significant, but I'd like to talk. I can be at your place in half an hour. Will that work?"

"That would be great."

"See ya then."

She headed for home, for the visit from Hawk. A visit without any interruptions from Brandon. Would he kiss her this time? Did she even want him to or would it just complicate things between them and make all their meetings after this uncomfortable?

It had been two years since she'd been kissed. Forever since she'd felt sensual passion.

Two years and forever had probably been long enough.

HAWK HAD TOLD THE TRUTH when he'd said there were no significant developments in the case. He hadn't been totally honest when he'd left out the fact that this wasn't just a personal call.

He hadn't exactly come to a dead end in the investigation, but at this point he was only retracing a journey the FBI had already mapped. He needed to chart a new course and to do that he needed to know exactly what had made her late husband tick. Where he hung out when he wasn't working or with her. Who he was afraid of. Who might have reason to hate him enough to kidnap his kid and torment his wife for years after his death.

His hunch after going over and over everything he'd gotten from Craig was that the villain might have no connections to Todd's professional life. The kidnapping and the cruel calls were as personal as it gets. The motivation for it might be as well.

So the purpose of this morning's visit was to pry into her personal life and question her about her relationship with her late husband.

She was just bound to love this.

He was settling behind the truck when he decided talking about this in Alonsa's cozy house would be exceedingly awkward. Fortunately, he had a plan.

ALONSA WAS WAITING at her front door when Hawk showed up pulling a horse trailer behind his truck. She stepped onto the porch. "Now you look like a real cowboy."

"I am a real cowboy. The morning's question is are you a real cowgirl."

She started to walk down to the circular drive where he'd parked the trailer. "You already know the answer to that."

"Tell me you at least know how to ride a horse."

"I'm a novice, but I've given it a shot."

He walked to the back of the trailer, unlatched the door and led out a magnificent cinnamon-hued mare with a flowing thick mane. "Meet Suzy Q. She's your mount for the morning."

"Oh, Suzy Q. You are a beaut," she crooned as she gave the horse a chance to get used to her.

The second horse was a beautiful black charger with a white patch down his nose and a belligerent snort.

"According to Linney, Suzy Q is the gentlest and calmest horse at the Double M," Hawk explained. "We'll take it easy and let you get acquainted with her and familiar in the saddle before we hit a gallop."

"So we just climb into the saddles and ride?"

"That's pretty much it. The horses do the rest of the work. Are you ready to go?"

She was wearing good jeans, a cashmere sweater and a pair of low-cut black dress boots, but why not? "Ready when you are."

Hawk handed her the reins, helped her onto the saddle, then checked the front cinch again. The nerves she'd felt while climbing atop Suzy Q settled quickly. She had ridden with Todd on several occasions. It had just been a while.

"This is your ranch," Hawk said once he'd mounted the stallion. "Any place in particular you'd like to check out on horseback?"

"There's a creek past the west pasture. I'm never sure exactly how to find it until I get close enough to see the branches of the big oaks that grow along its banks."

"Then let's head west."

He gave some rein and his horse trotted ahead. Suzy Q followed with no guidance from Alonsa. Not only was the mare gentle, she was smart, probably knew to keep up with the guy who'd brought her instead of depending on the female riding her.

In minutes, they'd settled into an easy canter and Alonsa's heart and breath had found a more rhythmical pattern. Rhythmical, but by no means calm.

The exhilaration only came in part from the ride. The rest was just the thrill of being with Hawk. Had someone told her before they'd met that she could be this intrigued by any man she'd have thought them crazy.

Even when she'd first seen him at the party, she'd taken him for a playboy. A gorgeous playboy, but certainly not one she'd want in her life. That was before he'd taken on the task of finding Lucy and then jumped in as if his doing it was the most natural thing in the world. And before the night in New York when he'd held her together while her heart had splintered like cracked ice.

They didn't talk, but she didn't mind. It was enough just riding alongside Hawk on a warm but overcast day in late January with the wind only a whisper in the grass and a gentle stroke on her face.

They cantered for a bit, then took the horses to a trot and later a full gallop before slowing to a canter again.

"The ranch is in good shape," Hawk said, finally breaking the easy silence he'd sustained for over a half hour. "A few of the fences need repair, but it wouldn't take much to get them in order. You could run a few hundred cattle easily on this spread."

"I don't know anything about raising cattle."

"You could learn. That's what Linney's doing.

Reading everything she can get her hands on and asking questions of the local ranchers. Cutter accuses her of worrying more about the horses and the herd she's building than she does him."

"Cutter exaggerates."

"He does, but still you could make it work here for you. Not that you necessarily should," he added. "It was just a thought."

She felt as if he were dismissing more than the conversation and was glad when the bare branches of the spreading oaks came into view. The creek had always been her favorite place on the ranch. The water was running fast and clear after the recent rains and she could hear it gurgle before they reached the spiny shadows of the trees.

Hawk dismounted, tied his horse then helped her do the same. They walked to the edge of the creek bed, stepping over muddy spots where the water was slow to drain. Two turtles slipped off a half-submerged log and splashed into the water.

"How do you know so much about ranching?" she asked.

"I was raised on one up in southern Oklahoma. My dad was the foreman. I helped from the time I was big enough to lift a pitchfork of hay."

"So you're not a pretender but a true cowboy."

"Whatever that means."

"According to Linney, it means a lot in Texas." Things like a love for the land they sweated for, keeping their word and never turning their back on a neighbor. It meant strong ties to their family and community and doing what was needed whenever it was needed.

"What made you leave the ranch and go into the service?"

"Got tired of the pitchfork and decided to see how a rifle felt."

He'd avoided the question. She should probably stop while she was ahead. But he knew all about her. She should know something of what made him who he was.

"Were your parents upset when you made that decision?"

"My dad was dead."

"I'm sorry."

He walked away, meandering down the banks of the creek bed without her but still in hearing range.

"What about your mother?"

"What about her?"

"Was she upset?"

"She hadn't bothered to come around in years, so I'm guessing she didn't really care what I did with my life."

Now Alonsa was really sorry she'd kept up with the questions.

"Come here and look toward that shrub on the other side of the creek," Hawk called.

Thankful to drop the subject, she walked over and did as he said.

"About halfway across the creek," Hawk said, pointing to the spot. "Just below the surface." He held on to her as she edged closer to the water.

She spotted the fish, staying in that one spot as if it were anchored, only its whiskers twitching in the moving water. "Is that a catfish?"

"One big enough to feed a crowd. You ever bring Brandon fishing down here?"

"I wouldn't know how to bait a hook."

"I could teach you and him."

The offer had a gravelly quality to it and suddenly Alonsa was all too aware of how close she was standing to Hawk and how his grip had tightened around her waist. She shifted so that she could see his face and look into his eyes. There was no mistaking the desire burning in their dark depths.

She pushed her body against his and wrapped her arms around his neck, burying her fingers in the thick locks of his hair. Finally, his lips found hers. The kiss loosed a rush of passion that ran hot and sweet inside her.

She thrust her body against him, sucked his breath into hers, trembled as his fingers splayed across her back and pulled her so close that she didn't know her heartbeat from his.

Her world began to spin. She'd forgotten that her body could burn like the sun had crawled into her chest. Or maybe it had never been quite like this.

Hawk's hands roamed her back while his lips crushed and possessed hers. Her lungs burned until she could barely breathe, and still she wanted more.

A RAW, POWERFUL HUNGER ripped through Hawk, his need becoming a raging fire that burned out of control. He hadn't planned this, but now that it had started, he knew just how badly he'd wanted it.

His tongue invaded Alonsa's mouth, tangling with hers. His hands slipped beneath the back of her sweater. Her bare skin was soft to his touch, warm and seductive. He couldn't get enough of her.

He pulled her to him, lifting her and letting her slide

down the throbbing length of him, his erection so hard his jeans could barely contain it. His chest was bursting, his mind reeling from the thrill.

He opened his eyes and scanned the area, intuitively searching for a place to lay Alonsa down on a carpet of leaves and soft grasses. A place where he could ravage every beautiful inch of her and find ways to fill her with pleasure and with him. The need was too strong to turn back now.

Thunder rumbled in the distance, low at first and then growling like rolling gunfire. The sound triggered a new level of alertness inside Hawk. He snapped to attention, the knowledge of what he was doing turning the fiery urges that drove him into pure agony.

Had he lost his mind? He couldn't throw Alonsa on the ground and make love to her like some animal in heat and then take her home to start drilling her about her private life.

The situation was just too damn invasive. Poor choice of words since invading her was exactly what he wanted to do. His entire body was in a state of massive sensual overload.

God, how he needed her. But not like this. Not when even before the passion had cooled, he had to start questioning her about her life with another man, the husband she'd lived with and made love to and had kids with.

He let his arms drop from around her and took a small step backward. His body felt stiff and exposed without hers pressing against it. The hunger for her was still pulsing inside him.

She stared at him, her expression impossible to read.

Then her eyes sparked angrily and he winced as if she'd slapped him.

It would have felt better if she had. Anyone who thought doing the right thing made a man feel good had never pulled away, in full heat, from a woman like Alonsa.

The thunder rumbled again, louder this time, and a streak of lightning zigzagged through the low hanging clouds. "Looks like those afternoon thundershowers the weatherman predicted are coming in early," he said. "We should get back to the house before it hits."

She stamped toward Suzy Q without answering or giving him so much as a backward glance.

They reached the house as the first drops of rain began to plop onto his hat. "Just in time," he said, dismounting and walking over to help her do the same.

She ignored his hand and slid to the ground on her own. "Do you need help getting the horses back in the trailer?"

"No, you stay dry. I can handle it."

"Fine." She turned and started toward the house, the heels of her short black boots slapping the driveway pavement.

Suzy Q neighed and pawed the ground.

"I know. I'm a horse's butt. Nothing personal." But he still had to take care of the business he'd come here to discuss.

"We need to talk, Alonsa." His voice sounded a lot sharper than he'd intended.

"Some other time," she called back. "I'm really busy now."

He swallowed hard. He'd changed all the dynamics

they'd had working for them, but he still had a job to do and a promise to keep. "It's about the investigation."

She stopped walking but still didn't turn around. "Okay. Let yourself inside when you're finished. I'll be in the kitchen."

Great, the nice, cozy kitchen while she glared at him and talked about her late husband, the famous FBI agent who'd probably never done anything wrong in his short life.

Chapter Eight

Rejection, pure and simple. After two years, Alonsa had put herself out there, and Hawk Taylor had said no, thanks. Only he hadn't bothered with the thanks.

There was no way she'd misread all the signals, definitely no way she hadn't felt his own hard need when he'd pressed his body against hers.

No way that sudden, precipitous dip in passion stemmed from the prospect of getting wet. He was a former navy SEAL, for cripes' sake! It wasn't like a little water would kill him.

But something had stopped him cold in his scalding hot tracks. He'd said he wasn't married but that didn't mean there wasn't a significant other. But if that was it, why not just come out and say it?

Another woman. That made sense. They were falling all over him at the party the other night. Maybe he'd followed up with one of them. Possibly Keidra Shelton. She was attractive, divorced and new to the area, having just moved to the Woodlands from somewhere in the Northeast.

Fine by Alonsa. She might have acted like a sex-starved bimbo at the creek, but she wasn't one. All she needed Hawk for was to find Lucy, so if Hawk wanted to talk about that, she was happy to oblige.

She glanced at the clock. But they'd have to talk fast. She had to leave here in forty-five minutes to pick up Brandon and she absolutely would not be late for that.

The doorbell rang. What part of *let yourself in* did the man not understand?

She'd kicked out of her muddy boots and left them on the porch and her neon purple socks peeked from beneath her jeans as she padded back to the front of the house. Her bright-hued socks and erotic panties were the two concessions she'd not made with her transition from flamboyant Broadway dancer to parenthood.

The front door was open wide. Hawk was standing just outside it, wringing a river of water from his shirt. Rain trickled from his hair to roll down his ears and neck and onto his broad, bare shoulders. His wet jeans clung to him. His naked toes wiggled on the drenched doormat.

Virility might as well have been tattooed across his damp, muscled chest.

Her insides did a belly flop that ended in a sharp, painful intake of breath. Where was her pride?

"You're drenched," she managed through a clogged throat. "I didn't realize it had started raining so hard." She'd been too lost in analyzing his rejection.

"I don't want to track water onto your floor. Can you get me a towel?"

"Right. Sure. A towel. Wait right here."

She returned a minute later with two large fluffy brown ones from the first-floor guest suite. She tossed them to him. "Anything else?"

"That should do it. I'm sorry to be so much trouble, but I came up with this theory and I need more information."

"Talk's not a problem, Hawk. The investigation is my first priority. And I'm not bothered by a few drops of water." She turned on a dime and marched back to the kitchen, ready to put the morning's rejection behind her and move on.

Finding Lucy was all that mattered.

CARNE WAS CURLED UP near the back door, sound asleep though his tail switched from time to time, no doubt missing his playmate. Alonsa stood at the sink, scraping carrots. Hawk straddled a kitchen chair, the wet jeans chafing a bit, but he'd endured a lot worse.

"I've gone over the entire list of reported sightings, including the ones that happened well after Lucy's disappearance," Hawk started, needing to get this over and done with since Alonsa had just given him a time limitation.

"I've also talked to a few of the people who called them in. As far as I can tell all the reports other than Marilyn Couric's were thoroughly checked out and proved erroneous. And I've gone over every scrap of info from Craig. At this point, I have to assume both the FBI and the HPD did a competent job of checking out other known suspects as well, though I'll go back to that if need be."

"So what is this new theory you mentioned?"

"It's the abduction itself and the calls you've received. Tonya Carrigan's photograph shows that Lucy was led from the zoo by a woman. Typically the fact that it's a female kidnapper rules out a sexual assault crime."

Typically, but not always. He was certain Alonsa knew that and this wasn't the time to throw that very sick possibility into the mix.

"There was no request for a ransom," Hawk continued, "which lessens the likelihood that this was either an orchestrated or random moment-of-opportunity crime for financial gain. And the telephone calls drastically reduce the possibility that the woman just found a lost child and decided to take the child to raise her as her own."

Alonsa finally turned away from the carrots and faced Hawk. "But that could have happened. The woman could be taking care of Lucy now as if she were her own daughter. Lucy could be safe and well cared for."

"I'm not eliminating the possibility that she's safe and well, but why torment you with those calls if all the kidnapper wants is anonymity?"

Alonsa washed her hands, dried them on a flowered cup towel and joined him at the table. "So we're back to the original theory of this being a grudge crime against Todd?"

He nodded. "But not necessarily one that had anything to do with his being an FBI agent. And not necessarily aimed at Todd."

"You think someone is trying to get back at *me* by kidnapping Lucy? That's absurd. What could I have ever done to anyone to make them hate me that much? No sane person would ever go that far."

"I didn't limit this to being aimed at you."

"Exactly what are you getting at, Hawk?"

"Just that paybacks in the world of drug cartels and

hardened criminals usually come in the way of a violent act with some kind of calling card, so to speak. That way there's no mistaking who's behind it. I'm sure the FBI has come to that same conclusion.

"Kidnapping, on the other hand, seems more personal. So do the phone calls. I just think it makes sense that whatever is behind those actions has to be personal, too."

She pushed her hair back from her face with both hands, keeping her fingers in place and squeezing her temples. Then the lines in her face and neck grew taut and she dropped her hands and collapsed into the kitchen chair catty-corner from his. "There are a lot of crazy people in the world."

"Too many," Hawk agreed. "That's why I need to know the personal details of your life, things that wouldn't be any of my business under ordinary circumstances."

"Things like whether or not I was sleeping with some other woman's husband when Lucy was kidnapped?"

"Yeah," he admitted, really glad now they hadn't made love back at the creek. It would make her think him even more the jerk.

"But this isn't limited to affairs or romantic triangles, Alonsa. I need to know everyone who might have reason to bear a serious grudge against you. Maybe someone you beat out for a juicy role on Broadway. Anyone who was unreasonably jealous of you for any reason, justified or not."

"Then why don't we start with my infidelities."

His stomach clenched.

"Sorry to disappoint you, but I was only sleeping with my husband at the time."

"I wasn't accusing you, Alonsa. It's that the investigation—"

She put up a hand to stop his apology. "Not a problem. You're just doing your job."

"What about the other aspects of your life?"

"This may sound naive, but I can't think of a single enemy I had in New York. I danced in chorus lines. We were competitive, but it was never any one person who beat you out of a chance. And at the time Lucy was abducted, I wasn't even performing."

She shook her head. "I'll give this some thought and get back to you, Hawk, but right now I can't think of a single person who'd go to such extremes to hurt me."

Which left Todd. He hated going there, but he'd crossed so many lines today, one more couldn't hurt. "Do you think Todd was unfaithful?"

And there it was, out in the open. The answer pooled in her dark eyes like melted snow. Thankfully this time the hurt and anger weren't directed at him.

"I think my husband was probably having an affair when he died. I don't have proof, but the signs were there. He'd stopped coming to my bed weeks before that. I'd talked to him about a separation but hadn't filed. It's hard to make that move when you have two young children."

She reached across the table and absently picked up a toy dinosaur from a line of them Brandon had likely been playing with at breakfast. She ran her index finger along the edges and then set it down in front of her.

"You're the first person in Dobbin that I've told about that."

"It won't go any further," he said. He fought the urge to cover her hands but it would have been too awkward after the morning's botched encounter.

"Todd and I had grown so far apart after I got pregnant with Brandon that I can't tell you much about his personal life."

"Who could?"

"Probably his lover, but I don't know her name. To tell you the truth, I don't want to know it. He's dead, and I only plan to pass along the good memories of him to his children."

"What about a close friend, someone not associated with the FBI?"

"Mitch Gavin," she answered quickly. "That was his best friend since college. They got together at least once a week. If anyone can tell you anything, it would be Mitch."

"Do you have his number?"

"I think so, or I can get it." She glanced at the clock on the wall oven. "Can I call you with that later this afternoon? I need to leave now to pick up Brandon."

"Sure thing. I'll just get my wet clothes and haul me and them out of your way."

After stopping at the counter to grab her keys, she followed him to the door. She picked up his soaked shirt while he retrieved his boots and socks. The rain had stopped and the sun had come out. Humidity clotted the air.

Their fingers touched when she handed him the shirt. She didn't back away and the moment grew tense.

"About this morning—"

"Brandon," she said, cutting off what would have

been a feeble attempt to explain his feelings and reactions when he didn't totally understand them himself.

All he knew for certain was that Alonsa had been hurt enough. If he could help it, he wasn't going to add to the pain. That didn't make it a damn bit easier to walk away.

CUTTER PITCHED SOME fresh hay into the barn's last stall, then hooked a foot on the stall door and stared at the black beauty staring back at him. Reaching the top slat, he scratched the snip of white beneath the soulful eyes.

Doing routine ranch work and helping his foreman, Aurelio, and his wranglers with the chores was Cutter's way of relaxing when his mind got too entangled in a case. Or when his vivacious wife threw him a curve he couldn't handle. That was happening more and more often these days.

"Okay, Lucy Lu," he said, bemoaning his concerns to Linney's favorite horse. "My wife spends more time with you than me, so what do you think is turning her into a water spout these days?

"Granted, I shouldn't have joked about making a saddle from her chicken fried steak last night, but that was only after she'd admitted it was indigestible.

"Cooking's not her thing. We both know that. Well, she's got spaghetti and meatballs down to where it's almost as good as Merlee's, but get past that and it's risky."

Lucy Lu snorted and threw back her head as if he'd just given her a horse laugh.

"Not funny, old girl."

Who cared if Linney wasn't a great cook? She was

dynamite at everything else she put her mind to. She and Aurelio had whipped the ranch into shape in no time flat. And the old ranch house had been spit and polished to a fair shine. Best of all, it looked and felt like home.

But then anyplace with Linney would be home. Her kiss made his morning. Her laughter highlighted his day. And crawling into bed beside her every night made life worth living. Always would. She claimed to feel the same way about him.

"So why all of a sudden turn into a broken water main every time the wind changes direction, Lucy Lu? Answer me that."

"You and Lucy Lu got a thing going on?"

"Just might," Cutter said, turning toward the barn door and the man standing in it. The fading sun backlit Hawk so that he looked more shadow than flesh and blood. From his stance, Cutter could tell something was weighing him down, too. "You going for a ride?"

"No. Aurelio said I could find you here. I wanted to check on the status of the case you've got coming up for me."

"I'm still working the deal," Cutter said. "Looks like it may be a couple of weeks before we come to an official agreement—if we come to an agreement. Lots of small print to work out when you deal with a government agency. They love regulations. I like to get the job done."

"I hear that."

"Have you heard anything from Goose about the sketch you gave him?"

"Not yet," Hawk admitted. "Hopefully he'll discover

the identity of the mystery woman, but I'm not counting too heavily on it."

"Do I detect a trace of uncertainty in your voice?"

"No uncertainty about the outcome, just the way I'm going to get there." He paused a mere second.

"Failure is never an option," he said, finally smiling and sliding back into the frame of mind that had seen Cutter and him through some hellish assignments as frogmen. They'd always come out with the mission accomplished. Hawk would find out what happened to Lucy.

Surely Cutter could handle a few overactive tear ducts.

"How are things with Alonsa?"

"She's hanging in there, eager to get her daughter back."

"I meant on a personal level."

"There is no personal level with us."

"Then why do I get the feeling that she's behind your lousy mood? My guess is you're falling hard for her."

Hawk shoved his hat back an inch or two off his forehead. "I have no idea what you're talking about."

"Yep. She's crawling under your skin, all right."

"You are obviously watching too many reality dating shows with Linney. And speaking of Linney, she just called and invited me to dinner tonight. Shall I bring the antacid for dessert?"

"No, I've got dozens of bottles hidden in my office. Just don't say anything like that to Linney. She's freaky sensitive about things these days."

"Really, 'cause she sounded in a great mood on the phone just now."

"A good mood? In that case, nice talking to you, pal, but duty calls back at the house." He looked around for his windbreaker and spotted it dangling from a peg a few stalls between him and the door, which Hawk was still blocking. He grabbed the jacket and scooted past Hawk. "Want some advice?"

"No, but something tells me the bullet's heading for me anyway."

"Don't fight it with Alonsa. Once they get inside you, you're doomed. If you don't believe me, ask Marcus." A few steps later Cutter stopped and looked back. "And pray for pasta."

CUTTER WAS WRONG. Hawk hadn't let Alonsa crawl inside him. He'd never let anyone delve into the old wounds, scars and sores that had been festering there for as long as he could remember.

He liked the fascia that covered little Tommy Taylor a lot better. Liked being Hawk. Liked being the brave navy SEAL people saw him as. Liked the respect that came with all that.

But the facade was only skin deep. The old wounds still lurked, ready to sink him like the deadly currents that lay hidden beneath the surface of a smooth sea. Let Alonsa crawl inside him and she'd back off faster than a man staring down a live grenade.

His cell phone dinged once, the signal he'd received a text message. He checked. The message was from Alonsa. Obviously she wasn't just dying to talk to him again.

Here's Mitch Gavin's cell number…

Hawk committed the number to memory as he went

back to the truck for his pen and notebook. Then he punched in the number and waited for an answer.

"Yo."

"This is Hawk Taylor. I'm looking for Mitch Gavin."

"You got him, but I don't recall ever meeting a Hawk Taylor."

"You didn't. I got your number from Alonsa Salatoya. I'm working with her to find her daughter."

"Are you with the FBI?"

"No. I'm with the Double M Investigation and Protection Service down here in Dobbin, Texas."

"So Alonsa finally went private. Couldn't understand why she didn't do that months ago. Todd would have. Actually, Todd would have found his daughter himself long before now. But that's a moot point, isn't it? How can I help you?"

"I'm running into a lot of dead ends. I think if I knew a little more about Todd's private life, I could get past some of them."

"I'm sure Alonsa can fill you in on the particulars concerning Todd."

Mitch's voice took on an edge that suggested he didn't like the idea of squealing on his dead friend. Hawk could understand that, but he couldn't accept it. "Wives don't always know everything."

"Did Alonsa tell you that?"

"No, that's just man to man, if you know what I mean. Besides, if Todd was half the father Alonsa says he was, I don't think he'd want anything he'd done to stand in the way of finding out what happened to his daughter."

"You mean find the perverted bastard that killed her, don't you?"

"There's no evidence she's dead."

"It's been two years. I know Alonsa can't bear to face it, but the kid's dead. Either at the hand of some perverted scum that picked her up at the zoo on a deranged whim or taken out by one of the subhuman forms of humanity Todd arrested. Some of those guys have no conscience."

"The subhumans in question have been investigated pretty thoroughly," Hawk said. "So have the perverts. And based on the evidence, I think the crime may have been on a far more personal level. Did Todd have anything going on in his private life that might cause someone to hold a serious grudge against him or Alonsa?"

"Todd? No way. He was a people person. Made friends of everyone."

"Was he having an affair?"

"Not at the time he was killed. He had been seeing a bimbo he'd met in a club down in SoHo, but they'd broken up a few weeks before that."

"Did his lover take the breakup bad?"

"Are you kidding? She dumped Todd for some TV producer. Best thing that could have happened to him. He decided it was time to grow up and start trying to make a go of his marriage. He was afraid Alonsa was serious that time about taking the kids and moving out."

"What about other women in his life?"

"He wasn't a hundred percent. He fooled around some, mostly just one-night stands."

Any guy fooling around on Alonsa had to be a hundred percent nuts.

"There was this one woman, pre-Alonsa. She was a real nutcase."

"In what way?"

"Stalked him when he went out with someone else. Called him all hours. You know, fatal attraction stuff."

"What happened?"

"I don't remember. She fell out of the picture a few years back. Guess she either met someone else to torment or moved away. No, wait, I think she checked in to a mental hospital. Come to think of it, Todd mentioned not too long before he was killed that she'd been in a car crash in New Jersey while high on prescription drugs. At least I think that was the same fruitcake."

"What was her name?"

"Damned if I remember. Michele, maybe. She was super smart, but got fired for some stupid reasons. Cool chick, but crazy."

"Did you ever meet her?"

"No. I was setting up a project in Australia when they were going hot and heavy. I saw a picture of her once. Not gorgeous, but not bad."

"Anyone else in his life who was that persistent?"

"No, but there was one woman who scared him," Mitch added. "Nothing personal about his connection with her, though."

"Who was she?"

"Some female attorney. He was working a case down in Houston."

Hawk's attention heightened. He poised his pen. "When was this?"

"Right before Todd was switched to the drug bust detail that got him killed."

"Do you know what kind of case it was?"

"Something about stealing babies and toddlers out of

Mexico and selling them to rich Americans who couldn't pass adoption regulations. Apparently the attorney ran the show, though she didn't get her hands dirty."

"What frightened him about her?"

"She was a mean friggin' bitch. One story said she'd ordered the murder of an entire family of some cop in one of the border towns. Three kids and a wife. Shot down like dogs. No proof it traced back to her, of course, but that was the rumor."

"Why did they pull Todd off the case?"

"No idea. But you can bet if they'd left him on the case, he'd have gotten the goods on her and put her away for life. He told her so. Pissed her off big time."

"Are you sure he never mentioned a name?"

"Like I said, Todd never gave out specifics. It wasn't ethical. You might use a little persuasion and get that name from Craig Dalliers."

Friendly persuasion was not Hawk's weapon of choice.

"I guess you've met Craig," Mitch said.

"I've talked to him."

"Really. How'd that work out for you?"

"He offered some cooperation." Apparently not nearly enough. He definitely hadn't mentioned a black-market baby ring.

"Craig must hate having another man on the scene. Probably green with jealousy."

"You mean because I'm stepping on his toes?"

"Because you're a new guy in Alonsa's life. He and Alonsa used to play footsies between the sheets, but you should probably ask Alonsa about that."

"None of my business."

"Whatever. Sorry I couldn't be more help, but you

take care. Like I said, Todd put some real mean sons of bitches away. You mess with them, they're liable to give you an early intro to your maker."

"I don't plan to let that happen."

"Neither did Todd. You know there's no real reason to tell Alonsa about Todd's infidelities. He loved her in his way."

"I'm not here to spread gossip. But I do have a sketch of a woman who might be connected to the abduction. Would you mind taking a look at it and see if you recognize her as someone Todd knew or had any kind of dealings with?"

"Can you fax it to me? I'm in my car now, but I'll check it out later."

"All I need's a number."

He wrote down that info as Mitch dictated it.

"I'll get back to you after I take a look at the sketch. When you see Alonsa again, tell her hello for me."

"Will do."

The idea of Alonsa having been with Craig in any kind of intimate way planted a rock-hard knot in Hawk's gut. Not only that, but if Mitch's accusation was true, then she'd lied about no one having a reason to hold a grudge against her.

Not that he suspected Craig's wife of kidnapping Lucy, but if Alonsa had lied about that, who was to say she hadn't lied about other affairs? The idea galled him to no end. Only why bother lying to him when she was desperate for him to find Lucy?

For now he'd give Alonsa the benefit of the doubt. In the meantime he'd follow Cutter's advice and pray for pasta.

And for the name of a Houston attorney with a black scrap of hell for a heart.

HAWK'S MIND WAS muddled with complications surrounding the fate of Lucy Salatoya when he walked from his two-bedroom cabin on the ranch to his pickup truck. A brown longhorn stuck its head over the top of a nearby fence and looked at him as if begging for a taste of the grass on his side of the barbwire.

Forbidden temptation was always sweeter, even to a steer.

He climbed behind the wheel and reached for his sunglasses. The sun's swan dive below the horizon could be brutal when you were driving west, even for only the half mile or so that separated his cabin from the main house where Cutter and Linney lived.

Hawk had moved in shortly after Marcus Abbot had moved out. He liked the feel of the place, rustic, cozy, lots of windows for soaking up the pastoral atmosphere.

Only place a man breathes free is on a ranch, his dad used to say. Hawk wasn't sure about that, but he did know ranching got in a man's blood, the same way being part of a Special Ops team did. Cutter had offered him a sampling of both. Live on the Double M and team up with him and Marcus in the business. The Double M Investigation and Protection Service. No boundaries. No limits. No job too tough.

The job he'd taken on himself wasn't too tough. Getting over Alonsa Salatoya might be.

He slowed as he approached the house. There was an extra car in the driveway. Alonsa's. Linney's matchmaking was in full swing.

Things bucked inside him, like his nerves were shorting out and recharging in random sequence. He doubted Alonsa would be thrilled to see him, but at least there would be no chance for a repeat of the kiss that had started the sensual onslaught this morning.

He might just get a few seconds alone with her to find out what kind of past she'd shared with Craig Dalliers. In fact, he was counting on it.

Chapter Nine

"I love your spaghetti and meatballs," Alonsa raved as she licked the last drop of spicy sauce from her lips. "I have to have your recipe."

"Did you hear that, loving husband of mine?" Linney cooed. "Alonsa wants my recipe."

"Can't blame her. The meal was magnifico!" He kissed his fingers in Italian fashion to punctuate his praise. "In fact, I think it was so fantastic that you and Alonsa should retire to the porch for coffee while Hawk and I clean up the kitchen. When we're through, we'll join you for dessert."

"Dessert," Hawk said. "Now you're talking."

"It's just lemon pie I picked up at a bakery in Conroe this afternoon," Linney confessed. "I didn't want to chance homemade since the last pie I baked we had to drink through a straw."

"But it was still delicious," Cutter said.

"Oh, you." She punched him playfully, but it was clear to Alonsa that she was drinking up his flattery. She loved watching their interactions. It was the way life should be between a husband and wife.

Fun and teasing, touching and caring. And passionate. She was certain that Linney and Cutter shared passion. Linney fairly glowed with it tonight.

Alonsa and Hawk had added the only tension to the dining room. This morning's kiss, and the way Hawk had broken off as if he were afraid it was going to contaminate him for life, had changed everything. And it wasn't as if she'd just thrown herself at him.

Well, she had, but it was clear he was as turned on as she was until… Until he wasn't anymore. So explain that.

"If it's okay with Alonsa."

Her name spoken in Hawk's voice jerked her back to attention. "I'm sorry. I was thinking of something else. Is what okay with me?"

"That you and I get a pass from KP chores."

She knew this was more of Linney's matchmaking but it had backfired on her friend this time. Hawk's only interest in Alonsa was in finding her daughter.

Which was more than enough and the best reason she could think of for retiring to the porch with him for a little private conversation. She wanted to know if he'd contacted Mitch and if the conversation had produced any information of value.

"I accept the offer to escape the kitchen," Alonsa acknowledged, "but I won't be able to stay late, no matter how good the pie. I promised Ellen I'd be home early."

"I'll get the coffee," Hawk offered.

Alonsa tried to help clear the table, but Linney all but pushed her out the door.

"You're wasting a full moon. And terrific weather, since the morning's thundershowers cleared out. Blizzards in half the country and sweater weather in Dobbin. I can't imagine living anywhere but here, especially when I have my own terrific cowboy."

No doubt Linney thought Alonsa needed one as well—in the form of Hawk Taylor. Linney had a serious lack of subtlety.

And a lot to learn about Hawk.

Alonsa left them all behind and settled on the porch swing to wait for Hawk. He joined her half a minute later, pushing out the front door and onto the porch with two green pottery mugs and napkins in hand. In spite of the rejection she'd felt this morning, her pulse accelerated.

He handed her a mug and a napkin. "I added a touch of Kahlúa and a dollop of whipped cream," he said. "I think I got the combination the way you like it."

She took a sip, then wiped the cream from her mouth. "It's perfect."

He took a seat beside her, not so close their knees touched but close enough that the musky scent of his aftershave vibrated through her senses.

"I didn't know you were coming tonight," he said, "but I'm glad you did. We need to talk."

"Did you get my text message this afternoon?"

"Yes, and I talked to Mitch."

"Did you send him the sketch?"

"I faxed it to him, but he was in his car at the time and I haven't heard back from him yet."

"Was he of any help in other ways?"

"He mentioned that Todd had broken off the affair he was having before he died and planned to give your marriage another shot."

"Thanks for sharing that, but Todd had made lots of

new stabs at making the marriage work. They never lasted long. He just wasn't ready to settle down, at least not with me. Anything else?"

"Mitch mentioned a black-market baby ring operating out of Texas that Todd had investigated. Did Todd ever mention that to you?"

"No, but like I told you, he seldom talked about his work. What about the baby ring?"

Alonsa listened and as Hawk fed her the details, her heart began to pound. The idea of stealing babies was too abhorrent for words, and the female attorney sounded like a deranged tyrant who should be shot at sunrise.

But if this lunatic was the one behind Lucy's disappearance, then Lucy might have been sold to a family who wanted an older child instead of a baby. She might be with a loving family who'd dried her tears and kissed her when she scratched her knee. Might have an illegally adoptive father who doted on her the way Todd had. Might have a substitute mother who combed her hair and made her chocolate chip cookies.

"This might be exactly the break we've been looking for, Hawk." Excitement bubbled inside her and spilled into her voice. "If the attorney is behind the abduction then there will be records. All we have to do is get our hands on them and we can follow the paper trail and find Lucy."

"Don't get your hopes too high, Alonsa."

Her enthusiasm plummeted. "Why do you always do this, Hawk? You assure me you will find out what happened to Lucy and then when we make progress you warn me not to expect too much. Are you going to do what you say you can or not?"

Hawk slid his arm to the back of the seat, snaking it behind her. "I didn't promise to do anything overnight."

"But this makes sense. We already know the woman took revenge on people who got in her way. And Mitch said that Todd wanted to take her down. And it was a woman who abducted Lucy. We know that much for sure. Now we just have to get to this attorney and we'll find Lucy."

"It's not as cut-and-dried as you're calling it, Alonsa, but it is worth checking out. The first thing we'll need is her name."

"Craig Dalliers must have it."

"In which case he knows about her and has probably already checked her out," Hawk said.

"He's never mentioned her. And he was looking for a person Todd had a part in arresting. As far as we know, this woman is still walking around Houston and running her sinful ring. She's unbelievably malicious and vindictive and even you said the person making those calls to me had to be cruel and heartless."

"I'm not arguing the point with you, Alonsa. I'm just saying I don't think you should put so much stock in every lead. It leaves you wide-open to disappointment over and over."

"I'm just trying to think positive. I'll get the name from Craig tomorrow."

"He may not be at liberty to release it to you."

"Oh, I'll get it, all right. Believe me, I have my ways, and I won't hesitate to do whatever it takes." She leaned back in the swing and took a slow sip of the coffee, this time relishing the sweet taste of the cream.

The chains squeaked as Hawk planted his feet firmly

and stopped the gentle sway of the swing. "I guess you'd be the one to know what it takes to get whatever you want from Agent Dalliers."

His tone was accusing. She turned and was surprised at the jut of his chin and the strained lines in his face. "Are you implying something, Hawk? If you are, don't beat around the bush, just say it outright."

"Okay. Mitch told me you and Craig shared a past."

"Did he now? A past? How thoughtful of him. And what did you say to that, Hawk Taylor?"

"That it was none of my business."

"You were right. It's none of Mitch's, either. But since my private life seems to be a hot topic of conversation, let me set the facts straight. I had an adulterous affair with Craig Dalliers."

HAWK REGRETTED ASKING before the first word of explanation left Alonsa's beautiful mouth. She didn't deserve this from him. Even if they were in a committed relationship, she didn't owe him a rundown of what she'd done before they met. But they weren't in a relationship of any kind. They'd shared one kiss and he'd done a rotten job of pulling that off.

"Let it go, Alonsa. Just hold on to the hope that this leads to our finding out what happened to Lucy."

"To our *finding* Lucy," she corrected him. "Not to finding out what happened to her. There's a difference." Her voice stung like a brutal wind. "And I'd rather get this out in the open so there's nothing between us but the search for Lucy."

"Fair enough." He damn sure wasn't going to go judgmental on her now.

"I dated Craig off and on for about six months before I met Todd."

"Then what happened?"

"He introduced me to Todd and Todd informed me that Craig was married. I broke it off with him immediately."

"Is that when you started dating Todd?"

"Yes. We fell hard and fast. Ours was the typical whirlwind romance."

"And Craig let it go at that."

"Hardly. He called me constantly trying to get back together. Todd finally threatened to call his wife if he didn't back off. Apparently she is a very jealous woman and inherited a rather large sum of money from an uncle who made it big in commercial real estate. Craig had no intention of leaving her. He just wanted me, as well."

"Did Todd's threat cause Craig to back off?"

"The threat and the fact that I got pregnant with Todd's child. I was taking precautions, but apparently my Lucy was meant to be. Todd wasn't ready to marry and start a family, but when I told him I was having the baby with or without him, he proposed."

The painful coils that had been twisting around the muscles in Hawk's chest began to relax. He was way out of line to even think about who Alonsa had been with before, much less to care.

Only he did care. Not about the past, but the here and now. He cared way too much and that scared him.

The door opened and Cutter and Linney joined them with slices of lemon pie piled high with a fluffy meringue. Hawk helped Linney with the tray, then propped himself on the banister with his dessert and what was left of his lukewarm coffee.

"Anyone for refills?" Linney asked. "It's decaf this time. I need my beauty rest tonight."

He held his mug up to be refilled, again reminded of how well Cutter and Linney fit together even if his buddy had been reduced to asking advice from horses a few hours earlier.

"Linney tells me this was Brandon's first day of pre-school," Cutter asked. "How did it go?"

"He loved it. He even asked to call Linney when he got home so that he could tell her all about it."

"He talked a mile a minute," Linney added. "I think he's majoring in blocks."

The pursuant conversation skirted several issues, none of which captured Hawk's attention. His thoughts were focused on Alonsa and the way she looked tonight. Casual dynamite, if he had to put a name to her style. She had on a pair of strappy heels that showed off her shapely ankles and made her legs look miles long. Her jeans fit just right. Her silky forest-green blouse was open at the neck, revealing a tasteful amount of cleavage.

But if they were alone and he were to loosen a few more buttons, the nipples that barely pushed against the fabric now would escape and her breasts would fall into his hands. He could kiss those soft, yielding lips again and...

His body hardened and blood rushed from his head, leaving him dizzy with wanting her.

"It's been fun, but I really have to go now," Alonsa said.

Hawk waited, still perched on the banister while the

others talked of getting together again soon and said their goodbyes. When Alonsa started down the steps, he followed and walked her all the way to the car before either of them said a word. When he looked back, he saw that Cutter and Linney had gone inside.

He opened Alonsa's car door. She didn't get in. He hesitated as the need he'd felt this morning rose inside him, pushing so hard it was all he could do not to take her in his arms.

"I didn't handle things well this morning, Alonsa."

She shoved the door open wider, knocking him backward. "We've covered this, Hawk. I came on to you. You weren't interested so you broke things off. I get it. I'm over it."

"You think I didn't want you? Are you crazy? I've wanted to make love to you ever since that first dance, maybe before."

"You have a funny way of showing it."

"I don't want to hurt you, Alonsa. I don't want to be the next man to let you down."

"Well, I'll tell you what I think, Hawk Taylor. I don't think this is about me at all. I think it's about you and your need not to get involved. So take that need and think about this."

He expected her to slap him. Instead she pressed her body against his and kissed him so hungrily, he had to hold on to the top of the car door to keep from falling backward.

The kiss ended as quickly as it had started. She pushed away from him and got into the car.

"Good night, Hawk. Now get busy and find my daughter."

With that she revved the engine and sped away, leaving Hawk to stare after her while he tried to wrap his mind around a woman who surprised him at every turn.

Unfortunately that didn't change a thing except to make what he had to do that much harder. Find Lucy, keep Alonsa safe and when this was over, walk away from the one woman he was certain he'd never be able to forget.

BOLTS OF UPHOLSTERY were fanned around the huge display table, all in the woodsy palette that Linney had used to update the furnishings in the main house at the Double M.

"I like this stripe for the chairs," Linney said, "and I like that leafy pattern for throw pillows, but I'm not sure they go together."

"The colors are all in your palette," Alonsa said, "but what do you think about this fabric with the trailing vines?" She moved that bolt to give Linney a better idea of what the two fabrics would look like together.

"I love it," Linney said, "especially the cranberry stitching."

"Agreed. Just the vibrancy you need to set everything off. You could also use this fabric to make more bed pillows."

They sifted through more fabric, and ten minutes later, Alonsa uncovered another match. "What about this for the corner table? It would go great with the brass bed."

"Oh, I love that. I don't know how you do it, Alonsa. I could have never pulled this together on my own."

"And I could never run a ranch the way you do."

"I have help. You could get good help, too, Alonsa. You could make your ranch a paying proposition in no time."

"I'm not sure I'll be staying in Dobbin."

"But you fit in so well here."

"I'm a New York girl."

"We don't hold that against you," Linney teased. "You could settle down with a gorgeous cowboy. I wholeheartedly recommend it."

A cowboy like Hawk Taylor. She knew what Linney was thinking but she wasn't going there. She hadn't seen or talked to him since she'd thrown herself at him for the second time the other night at Linney's.

She hadn't planned to kiss him like that. He'd just gotten her so exasperated. It wasn't that she expected him to jump her bones every time they were together, but he didn't have to make such a point of backing away from her.

She might not be an authority on men, but there was no denying the sparks that flew between them. Even Hawk had admitted that.

So the only explanation she could think of for his actions was that getting involved with her would cramp his style.

The search for Lucy was getting more than a little exasperating as well. This time it was Craig who was causing the bottleneck. She'd called him repeatedly, leaving messages that it was urgent she talk to him. He had yet to return her calls.

Either he was extremely busy, as his secretary insisted, or he was blowing her off. She suspected the latter.

Gathering her selected fabrics, she led Linney to the counter.

"I'll give the clerk the measurements and have her ring it up. She can cut it later and I can come back for it."

"Right. I guess you do need to get back to Dobbin. I forget Brandon is in the church preschool now."

"He got up this morning raring to go. I'm starting to feel a little neglected."

"Tomorrow's Saturday. You'll get your turn with him. Why don't you bring him over? He loves the horses."

"We'll see."

The horses would be great but going to the Double M also meant the possibility of seeing Hawk and she wasn't sure she was ready to jump into that again after the way they'd parted. At least not until she heard from Craig and they had something pertaining to the search to discuss.

"If you don't mind, I'm just going to collapse in that chair over there while you talk to the clerk," Linney said. "I'm pooped."

"You're not sick, are you?"

"No. I guess I've just been trying to do too much lately. I'll be fine. I just need to rest a minute."

"You do so much you make the bionic woman look like a slacker, but I've never seen you with your battery running on low before."

Linney yawned and dropped into the chair. "Guess it's catching up with me. I'll be here when you're ready to go."

"Okay. I won't be but a minute or two."

It would have only taken a minute or two except that both clerks were busy with other customers. Meanwhile Alonsa checked her phone for missed calls.

None. Moving away from the counter, she punched in Craig's cell phone number. No answer. Her irritation surged. "This is Alonsa again. Either call me back before noon, Craig, or expect to find me sitting on your front doorstep when you get home tonight. And, no, I am not kidding."

She was bluffing, but another day of waiting and she might make good on it.

"Alonsa, what a surprise."

Her latest client appeared at her elbow.

"Keidra. Good to see you."

"You, too. I was just browsing so I'll have some idea of what fabrics are available before we meet. I talked to Esteban earlier today and told him I'm ready to start redecorating when you guys are. The previous owners had simply horrid taste."

"Sounds good. I'll get back to you early next week."

"Perfect. How's your son?"

"He's fine. The bump was nothing."

"Good, but I know how we mothers worry. I have a daughter."

Alonsa didn't mind hearing about Keidra's daughter, but she'd do it on Keidra's time. The clerk had become available.

Back down to business, she checked out and in no time she and Linney were on their way home. Traffic was light on 105 and they got back to Dobbin in under twenty minutes. There was no sign of Hawk when she dropped off Linney.

She left and went straight to the church. She was early so she got out of her car to sit on an intricately carved bench beneath a canopy of bare branches while she waited. It looked to be a peaceful spot. The effect was lost on her, though.

Her phone rang. Craig was on the line.

Chapter Ten

Alonsa quickly explained the situation with the Texas attorney.

"Where did you get this information?" Craig demanded, clearly not pleased.

"Does it matter?"

"The Bureau's involvement with that case is confidential."

"I'm not at liberty to say where I heard about it, but that's not the point."

"It is exactly the point, Alonsa. I can't discuss any part of that investigation with you."

The little patience she had was fast running out. "This attorney could be involved with Lucy's disappearance. We need to act on it immediately."

"By we, I assume you mean you and that soldier cowboy posing as an investigator."

So that's what his attitude was about. He was still angry that she'd brought Hawk in on the case.

"There is no way I can turn over confidential information to you or Hawk Taylor, especially when it doesn't concern your daughter."

"How can you be sure it doesn't? Did you ever consider that this woman may have had Lucy abducted and sold on the black market?"

"In the first place, Alonsa, there is no credible evidence tying anyone in Houston to a baby theft ring. If there were, that person would still be under investigation making it even more imperative that I not leak details about the situation. In the second place, there's no credible evidence that such a ring operates in this country."

This wasn't working. She should have gone to New York and talked to Craig face-to-face. Since she hadn't, there had to be a way to get through to him.

"I know Todd was on the case, Craig. The attorney exists. If nothing else, just give me her name."

"Let it go, Alonsa. If Todd was on such a case—and I'm not confirming that he was—he was removed from the investigation due to lack of evidence. Considering that and the fact that he was already dead at the time Lucy went missing, what possible reason would this attorney you're talking about have for abducting Lucy?"

"Because Todd believed she was guilty and he told her he was going to take her down."

"And how would you know that?"

"I just do. And the woman's incredibly vindictive. She killed a man's entire family just because he crossed her. What's one abduction to a woman like that?"

"Do you have proof of any of this?"

"Just give me the attorney's name, Craig. You've said yourself time after time that you'd do anything to help me get Lucy back."

"And I will, Alonsa. I'll look into this myself, I promise. But I can't flagrantly disregard Bureau policy."

She had a few suggestions for what he could do with his Bureau policy. It was a struggle not to hurl them at him. She would have if she'd thought they would help. She *had* to have the name of that attorney.

"You know how I feel about you, Alonsa, how I've always felt about you. Fire that bozo and come back to New York where I can see you. I'll work with you personally on this."

Her stomach roiled and her resolve turned to solid steel. "Give me the attorney's name, Craig, or I'll go to your wife and tell her about our affair. I'll give her names and dates and details. And then I'll tell her how you've hit on me constantly since Todd's death."

"Don't be ludicrous. You know you wouldn't do that to me or to Ginny. You're letting Hawk call the shots. I'll bet he's there right now listening to every word you say and egging you on."

"The name, Craig, or I hang up this phone and call Ginny right now. Don't push me because I'm ready to break. I want my daughter back and if that costs you a divorce, then that's just the way it is."

Noises came through the phone as if he were choking or gasping for breath. He could be having a heart attack. Her breath balled in her throat.

"You bitch, and after all we've meant to each other."

Apparently he hadn't had a heart attack. He had no heart. "The name, Craig."

"You'll regret this."

She waited.

"Caroline Wardman, but if this gets out, I'll swear on a stack of bibles you didn't get it from me."

Alonsa's hands shook as she broke the connection and punched in Hawk's number, praying that this was finally the break that would bring Lucy home.

ALONSA HAD ASKED Hawk to give her an hour to get Brandon fed and down for his nap. He'd obliged and kept busy every second, researching Caroline Wardman.

The attorney had an office in the Heights, a community near downtown Houston just north of Buffalo Bayou. According to his research it was an area of older homes, many of which had been restored. A few had been turned into offices.

Her age was fifty-two, or fifty-six, depending on which site you believed. She had served on several cultural arts boards and hosted numerous political fundraisers. A wealthy woman with clout. Easy to understand why the FBI hadn't gone after her without solid evidence of wrongdoing.

Needless to say there was no indication that she was engaged in illegal activity or had ordered anyone killed. She did specialize in assisting with foreign adoptions but her practice was not limited to that.

She'd be a hard nut to crack. That didn't deter Hawk. Challenges made life interesting. But to him this was another avenue to be explored in the search for Lucy Salatoya.

As always, it was more than that for Alonsa. Her spirit lived and died with every lead, and he dreaded watching her plunge into despair if this didn't work out. Caroline Wardman was a long shot at best.

He drove up in front of Alonsa's house at five minutes after one knowing that he'd have to work to keep her expectations within the bounds of reality.

Hers were not the only expectations he'd have to watch. He'd spent far too much time reliving the passion they'd tasted down by the creek and the fury-fired kiss she'd left him with that same night.

Every sane thought reminded him that making love with her would put them on a slippery path to disaster. There was nowhere for the relationship to go. Alonsa would want more than he could give. She deserved more.

He embraced the self-lecture as he walked to her door. His resolve transformed into rapid-fire blasts of arousal the second she opened it.

She was wearing her hair different, pulled up on top of her head with wispy tresses escaping the knot. The front slit in her straight black skirt showed enough smooth thigh to make his mouth water. Delicate silver hearts dangled from her earlobes and called attention to the smooth column of her regal neck.

Finally, he let his gaze focus on those full, tempting lips that had the power to knock him totally off his feet. Not wise to trust his instincts with Alonsa today.

He had to play this cool.

He managed a hello that he hoped revealed none of what he was feeling. He followed her to the family room. The view from the back was equally as devastating.

There was no sign of Brandon or Carne, but there was a cheeseboard laden with several varieties of cheese, slices of apple and pear and a bowl of wheat crackers. A tray sitting next to it held napkins and cups waiting to be filled with drink from colorful carafes.

"Are we celebrating?" Hawk said, helping himself to a hunk of cheddar.

"I wasn't sure you'd had time for lunch and I didn't want us to stop for food until we'd had time to map out our strategy."

He chewed and swallowed. "Sounds good except for that little word *our.* I work alone in my capacity as investigator. Did I not mention that?"

"I got the name of the attorney," she reminded him, as if that meant he owed her. "There's coffee or hot tea. Which would you prefer?"

"A cold beer." He figured he'd better veer from her ground rules before this went too far and she really believed she was going to have a say in the strategy.

"I'm sorry. I don't keep it on hand. I have wine."

"Not a problem. I have a six-pack in a cooler in the back of my truck. How about you? Can I get you one?"

"I suppose, if you're going outside anyway."

"Two beers coming up."

He sauntered back to the truck and got three while he was at it. He had a feeling he was going to have a fight on his hands and might need the fortification. Granted, Lucy was Alonsa's daughter, but his methods weren't up for a popular vote.

If it turned out Caroline Wardman was behind Lucy's disappearance, they'd be dealing with a powerful, vindictive woman and he was taking no chances with Alonsa's safety.

When he returned with his beverage of choice, they went over the facts that they knew for certain. It all boiled down to Caroline Wardman being an attorney who specialized in foreign adoptions who had once been investigated for possible involvement in a baby smuggling ring.

The investigation had been called off due to lack of evidence. And she might have been threatened by Todd. They only had Mitch Gavin's word on that.

Hawk helped himself to more cheese and a handful of the mini crackers and washed it down with a swig of beer. "I appreciate your getting the name, Alonsa. I'll keep you posted as to how this progresses."

She shot him a look that was painfully void of sensuality. "I'd like to know your plan of action."

"I'm thinking I'll just get a bunch of my buddies together and we'll pick up some AK-47s and storm her office with bullets blazing."

"You can't do that. It's—" She exhaled sharply. "This isn't funny, Hawk. We're talking about my daughter. This woman knows where Lucy is. I'm sure of it. We can't make mistakes."

"Okay, calm down. I don't have a game plan yet. I'm Special Ops trained. We check out every element of a mission before we dive in. Surprises do not make for happy endings."

Alonsa crossed her shapely legs. "How will you check out these elements?"

"The old standby, snooping. I'll find out everything I can about the attorney and her background. Then I'll make an appointment and meet her on her turf. That way I can get a look at her operation. I don't try to judge a book by its cover, but I can tell a lot about people just by observing them in their own little fishbowl."

Alonsa set the beer she'd been nursing on the edge of the tray. "Make an appointment to do what?"

"Talk to her about adopting a baby from Mexico. I'll see what kind of information she gives me and who she hooks me up with. Then I'll go from there."

"Good idea. I'll go with you."

"Bad idea."

"I don't see why. It's not like you could adopt a baby by yourself. You need a wife or rather someone to play the part of your wife."

"You're Lucy's mother and Todd's wife. If the honorable attorney is behind the abduction and the phone calls, she'll recognize you."

"Not if I go in disguise. I can wear a wig and glasses, big-rimmed glasses. And I'll use stage makeup. I know how to add acne scars to my face. I had to do that before when I played a wicked old hag in a show."

Talk about your screwed casting.

"I had moles with long hairs protruding from them as well," she continued, "but that's probably taking things a bit too far."

"A bit."

"I even know how to dress so that I look twenty pounds heavier. I can do it, Hawk. I know I can. You won't even recognize me. And I need to be there. I'll hear or see something that will help us find Lucy. I feel it deep inside me."

"I'd need to spend the night," he said, "to check the lay of the land after dark and determine what it would take to pull off a successful break-in."

"I could find someone to watch Brandon for one night. Linney or Ellen, or even Merlee. We can get two rooms, and except for when we meet with Caroline Wardman, you won't even know I'm there."

It would take considerably more than glasses, acne and twenty extra pounds for that. When he needed his wits about him most, he'd be distracted by considerations for her safety. And he didn't even want to think about the stress of controlling his sensual cravings with them staying in the same hotel.

"I'll think about it, Alonsa." Which was better than arguing with her.

"I can be ready to go tomorrow."

"I can't. I'll get back to you when everything is a go. We'll talk then."

She stood and her mouth drew into a tight line, her gaze piercing. And then she delivered the clincher.

"Okay, Hawk, you decide whether or not you want me to go with you or if you'd rather I go to see Caroline Wardman by myself."

He groaned. Just like in the military, the easy way was always mined.

THE WOMAN WOKE to a house that was pitch dark, not even a glow from the hall night-light to illuminate the shadows. The electricity must have gone out during the night. She hated the dark. It made her shaky. Her nerves were a mess as it was.

She kicked off the covers and reached in the drawer beside her bed for her flashlight. Her fingers brushed the tiny thin metal key. She clasped it and pulled it from the drawer. It slipped from her fingers and she slid off the edge of the bed and onto her knees, fumbling until she recovered it.

Aiming a narrow beam of light into the darkness, she padded to the bathroom, reached to the top shelf of the linen closet and unlocked the metal file box. The pills were in the front corner, locked away so no one would see them or ask about them. She held the bottle, unscrewed the lid and poured two round white pills into the palm of her left hand.

They were getting harder and harder to come by. The doctors were nervous these days about writing prescriptions for mood-altering drugs. Too many side effects. Too many lawsuits, or so they claimed. She swallowed the pills then turned on the faucet and cupped her hand beneath the spigot, collecting enough water to make the drugs go down easily.

In the old days, she'd injected it directly into her vein. That was before she'd made the horrifying decision that haunted her still. That night, she hadn't been the one holding the needle.

Pushing her fingers to the back of the file box, she located the CD. Her hand rested on top of it, but she didn't pick it up. Its days of bringing her satisfaction were soon to come to an end.

One more little surprise and then Alonsa would pay the ultimate price for what she'd stolen. It had always been the plan and now everything was falling into place.

It would be the perfect gift for the little girl whose birthday would never come.

Chapter Eleven

The appointment with Caroline Wardman was set for Tuesday morning. By the time Hawk and Alonsa drove to Houston on Monday afternoon, Hawk had heard back from Mitch. He thought the woman in the sketch looked vaguely familiar, but he couldn't place her.

If the sketch had been more distinct he might have been able to help, or so he'd said. He'd promised to give it more thought.

Hawk had also collected enough information to conclude that while Caroline Wardman's business methods would likely not win her any awards for ethics, she probably wasn't doing anything entirely illegal, either.

Yet she'd caused enough waves that the FBI had her investigated, so he wasn't ruling anything out. All you had to do was listen to the evening news to know that the world was full of people who pulled the wool over everyone's eyes—until they were caught.

Caroline Wardman could turn into a case in point, which was why Hawk had given in to Alonsa's insistence that she come with him for tomorrow morning's appointment. If he hadn't, she would have made good on her word to visit the attorney on her own.

In spite of the evidence he'd collected, Alonsa still had high hopes that they were about to discover the yellow brick road that would lead them to Lucy.

At Linney's suggestion, he'd booked rooms for them at a bed and breakfast in the Heights area, just a few blocks from the attorney's office. His treat this time, although Alonsa had balked at his not letting her pick up expenses as they'd agreed on initially.

But a woman who tangoed through all his dreams and whose kisses haunted his every waking moment shouldn't pick up the tab for his room.

The B and B was a sprawling turn-of-the-century house filled with antiques and smelling of lilacs. To call it romantic would be a gross understatement. The place reeked of it. And temptation was only a door away.

Not that he had any plans for a midnight seduction. Nothing had changed between them. Alonsa was still vulnerable. He was still bad news in jeans and neck deep in this investigation.

He was meeting her for dinner in a matter of minutes and for once it would be much appreciated if she didn't look so damned irresistible.

He stuffed his wallet in his pocket, grabbed his sport coat and turned out the light, closing and locking his door behind him. Alonsa's door was open. He tapped anyway.

"You decent?" *Please be.*

"Hawk, glad you're here. I need some help with this zipper."

She waltzed out of her bathroom in a black dress

with a skirt that swung enticingly just above her knees and a pair of gold stiletto heels that did mind-boggling things for her shapely legs.

The real killer was when she turned her back to him. The zipper had gotten stuck just above her waist and her bare back glistened in the glow of the lamps. She wore no bra.

Every part of him reacted to the sight. Playing it cool was no longer an option. He shrugged out of his jacket, crossed the room and took her in his arms. When his lips found hers, and she kissed him back, he knew that dinner was going to be very, very late.

ALONSA MELTED INTO the kiss and her mind grew giddy with the thrill of it. She'd tried to talk herself out of wanting Hawk this way after his rejection, had worked to convince herself she didn't need him or his kisses. The denial dissolved the second his lips touched hers.

Her body vibrated now with a need so intense she couldn't think or reason. Her pulse was racing, her heart beating to a rhythm that rocked her soul.

Hawk's mouth left her lips and seared a wicked hot trail down her neck. The slow burn was maddening and hot flushes ran rampant through every cell of her body. Her head swam. Her heart felt as if it were on the verge of bursting from her chest.

She knotted her fingers in his hair, pulled him closer while his lips pushed away the loose neckline of her dress and kissed their way down her bare chest. Her nipples grew erect and hard, pulsing and pointing, begging for more as his tongue teased and his lips nibbled and sucked.

She needed this so badly, needed Hawk with his virility and determination, his smile and his strength. Needed to unleash the swirl of wanton emotions that were coursing through her. She needed passion.

He slipped his right hand beneath the skirt of her dress and slid it between her thighs, slowing working his fingers upward until they dipped inside her panties and rolled across the sweet core of her desire. The intensity of the pleasure became liquid fire. She ran her hand down his body, gingerly massaging the hard length of his erection.

"Make love with me," she whispered. "All the way. You inside me. Me pleasuring you. Without all those clothes you have on."

"Oh, Alonsa, there's no way you couldn't pleasure me. I'm so crazy for you right now, I can barely breathe."

"Then take me any way you want."

He pulled away and put both his hands to the task of rescuing her from the stuck zipper. The wait was pure torture.

"It's not budging." Frustration and desire graveled his voice.

"Rip it off, Hawk. Please, just rip it off. I have plenty of dresses."

He gave a quick jerk. "Mission accomplished," he announced as it pooled at her feet. He tucked a finger inside the waistband of her lacy purple panties. "What about these?"

"You decide."

"That's a no-brainer." He slipped them down her legs, slowly while he kissed her most intimate areas, driving her into ecstasy all over again.

"Your turn," she said. "I want to undress you."

She unbuttoned his shirt and slipped it off his shoulders, but then the hunger rocked through both of them and he wiggled out of his jeans and boxers on his own. Once done, he lifted her and carried her to the bed.

She kicked back the quilt and rolled onto the lilac sheets and into his arms. The passion was already at a fevered pitch and when Hawk raised and straddled her, she cradled his erection in her hands and guided him inside her.

He thrust hard and deep, building to a crescendo until the explosions began. Rockets and starbursts and red fiery flares. She trembled and cried out as he carried her to the most intense orgasm she'd ever known.

When his breathing slowed and he rolled away, he pulled her against him and held her close.

There were no whispered mutterings of love, but she'd never felt this much a part of anyone before. She found it hard to believe she ever would. Whatever came of their relationship, she would never be sorry for tonight. Hawk Taylor was a man among men in every way.

More man than even she'd suspected. She was still basking in the sweet afterglow of passion when he was ready to go again.

HAWK WOKE AT THREE in the morning to the gentle, rhythmic sounds of Alonsa's breathing and a niggling ache between his legs. He stared at the ceiling, letting the scintillating memories sift through his mind.

They'd made love three times last night, twice before dinner. Once more after they'd eaten at a nearby restaurant and then walked to the attorney's office to scope out the lay of the land by night.

He hadn't planned to make love with Alonsa last night, but he wasn't sorry that he had—at least not yet. How could he regret having his body and soul climb to places he'd had no idea existed?

He wondered now if that deep connection was what real love was all about. He'd never really thought that much about it before, had no basis for recognizing it. He did know what had transpired between them had been on a level that was new and totally unfamiliar to him.

He reached over and tangled a finger in her hair. He fought the desire to stroke her beautiful breasts and the softness of her belly.

He imagined waking up with her morning after morning, desire running hot between them, her laughter and dark, hypnotic eyes sparkling in the first rays of the sun.

Yeah, right. It would be just like that. In a dream world. Hawk didn't even have the address of that planet.

He slid his legs over the side of the bed, slowly, careful not to wake Alonsa. He was wide-awake but there was no reason to disturb her. He pulled on his boxers, gathered the rest of his clothes and let himself out. He locked the door behind him and then slipped the thin metal key back under her door.

Leaving her lying naked in bed just might be the hardest thing he'd ever done, and he regretted the act before he reached his own door.

THE HOUSE THAT Caroline Wardman had chosen as her place of business was a study in contrasts. The outside was a refurbished, Victorian mansion. Wide porches. Two turrets. Intricate gingerbread trim.

The inside was twenty-first-century posh with a bit of new age asceticism thrown in for effect. Plush carpets. Expensive etched-glass chandeliers. Abundant leather furnishings and stark black and white lamps and vases.

Alonsa took a seat in the back of the high-ceilinged waiting room and leaned over to whisper in Hawk's ear. "The attorney could use a good interior design consultant."

"You could volunteer."

"That's not a bad idea," Alonsa said.

"I was only kidding."

"I'm not. If I hung around here, I could surely gain access to her files."

"Don't even think about it."

She guessed it would be a waste of time after the comment Hawk had made last night when they were prowling in the dark. He was certain he could disarm the alarm system and let himself into Caroline's inner sanctum with no one the wiser.

Last night. Heated memories returned in a dizzying, frustrating rush. They'd made love for the third time and then sometime in the night or early morning hours he'd crawled out of her bed to go back to his own.

She'd been irritated at what she viewed as renewed rejection when she'd first woken and found him gone. She'd gotten over that quickly enough when he'd shown up a bit later with a bagel and coffee and kissed her good morning.

And that kiss came after she'd added some rather scary acne scars to her cheeks and forehead.

He was as full of contrasts as this house. More complex. A million times more exciting. He was all business now and she felt a renewed sense of confidence that a major breakthrough was on the horizon. She prayed it would be today and she couldn't wait to actually meet Caroline Wardman.

But wait they did for thirty long minutes before they were ushered into the attorney's office. The woman didn't look up when they entered but kept talking on the phone and letting condensation from a glass of what appeared to be grapefruit juice drip onto a 4 X 6 photograph of a newborn.

The crass woman was capable of the worst crimes against human nature. Alonsa was certain of it.

HAWK STARTED SIZING UP the attorney the second they walked into her private office.

"I'm sorry to keep you waiting," she said, finally hanging up the phone and turning her attention to them. "It's been a hectic morning. One of our adoptive mothers who was supposed to pick up her baby today had an accident on the drive home from work last night and is in the intensive care unit. It throws the paperwork into a tailspin."

"What happens with the baby?" Hawk asked.

"He stays on with Social Services. But don't worry, if that mother doesn't work out, the agency I represent has a waiting list of prospective parents. Now how can I help you?"

"We're interested in adopting," Alonsa said, even though Hawk had warned her to let him do the talking.

He had to hand it to her disguise talents, though.

He'd have recognized her sexy walk and the fragrance she wore, a flowery scent that always threw his libido a curve, but her appearance would fool ninety-nine and nine tenths percent of the people who knew her.

"I don't know how you got my name," Caroline said, "but you've come to the wrong place. I merely handle the paperwork. You'll need to visit the agency's office on Main to file for adoption. I can give you their phone number and address."

"It's the paperwork that concerns us," Hawk said. "How do we know for certain the biological parent can't come back and claim the baby after we've paid all the money and grown attached to the infant?"

"The contract's ironclad. They sign away all their rights."

"But what happens if they try to get out of the contract?"

"They're never given the names of the adoptive parents. They'd have no way of tracking you down. But if you're still worried, you should talk to the agency. I'm sure they can address any concerns you might have."

"Where do they store all this paperwork? Is it somewhere the real parent can't just look it up on the Internet?"

"If you adopt a child, you are the real parent. And I can assure you the files are confidential and not accessible via the Internet. They're under lock and key at the agency."

"Then you don't store them here for safekeeping?"

"Not once they're completed and all parties have signed off on them."

Which meant there wasn't any reason to break in to

her office, though from what he'd noted, it would be a
fairly easy task. He pretty much had what he'd come
for. The woman was in this to make money and
appeared to be doing a good job of that. He didn't see
her as the mastermind of a baby theft ring, but he could
be wrong.

He opened his notebook for an additional test now
that he didn't see how he had anything to lose by
angering the attorney.

"I have a confession to make," he said. "We're not
really looking to adopt a baby. I'm a private detective
and I'm trying to track down this woman's sister." He
nodded toward Alonsa. "She thinks her sister may have
adopted a baby from the agency you represent and it's
important that she locate her."

Alonsa uncrossed her legs and stared at him from
beneath her mousy wig.

Caroline glared at him openly. "You've wasted your
time, Mr. Taylor or whoever you are. Anything I know
is protected by client privilege."

"Just take a look," he urged. He took Marilyn
Couric's sketch from the notebook and pushed it onto
the back of her desk.

Caroline didn't pick it up, but he watched closely as
her gaze shifted to the sketch. There was absolutely no
visible reaction on her part. That settled it in his mind.
She had not hired that woman to abduct Lucy.

They were back to square one. For Alonsa, it would
be a long ride back to Dobbin.

THEY RETURNED TO THE B and B just long enough to
pick up their luggage and for Alonsa to shed the wig,

wash the scars from her face, put on fresh makeup and change into something more becoming than the drab suit that had made her look downright pudgy. He had no idea how she'd accomplished that.

Hawk opted to hang out in the back flower garden with the owner, who was adding some bulbs to two of the beds. If he'd gone back to Alonsa's room while she was changing clothes, he might have wound up paying for an extra night.

Not that he'd mind, but Alonsa was already antsy to get back to Dobbin and pick up Brandon from the Double M. He could tell she was trying hard not to let her disillusionment with the morning's outcome show, but he knew her too well to be fooled. She was so desperate to find her daughter that any disappointment hit her hard.

Two years of waiting, worrying, hoping and praying with nothing but heartache for her efforts. He didn't know how she did it. A mother's love. Women like his mother were obviously missing the gene that enabled it. Alonsa must have been blessed—or cursed—with a double supply.

The man in the earth-stained overalls stood and swiped his hands across the bibbed front. "The missus says you're from Dobbin."

"I am. Just moved there, though."

"You like it?"

"I'm learning to."

Up until now he hadn't enjoyed it nearly as much as he'd enjoyed his evening in the Heights. He was still reeling from the thrill of making love to Alonsa and couldn't wait to do it again. They would, he knew. They'd crossed a line and there was no going back.

None of the reasons for avoiding it had changed, but making love to Alonsa was like a drug habit that he'd never be able to break. He wouldn't have to. Sooner or later, she would.

He talked a few minutes more to the owner then said a quick goodbye when he spotted Alonsa carrying her bag of stage makeup and fake hair to the truck.

The owner spotted her too. The guy was probably pushing seventy and openly ogling. "Nice-looking woman. You're a lucky man."

"Damned lucky." For now.

AFTER THIRTY MINUTES of rehashing the morning's meeting with Caroline Wardman, Alonsa chose a CD from Hawk's case and inserted it in the truck's dashboard player. Keith Urban's voice came at them in stereophonic sound.

She tugged on her seat belt and shifted in her seat. "I think Texas is growing on me."

Hawk smiled but kept his eyes on the road. Afternoon traffic heading north on I-45 was a bitch. "Did I hear that wrong or did Miss New York just admit to getting turned on to the Lone Star State?"

"It's not the Big Apple but it has its own charm. It's quieter, especially on the ranch. The winters are great. And Texans are so friendly it's hard not to feel at home among them."

"You certainly hit it off with Linney."

"She's a terrific friend, the closest I've had since high school."

"That says a lot."

"It does. High school was a blast. College, not so

much. I was set on being a dancer by then and studying seemed a total waste. I left the University of Arizona midway through my junior year and headed to New York."

"That must have incurred some flack."

"Dad was livid, but he came around when he saw me in my first Broadway chorus line. Mom always understood. And then I gave it all up for marriage and kids and you know the rest of the story."

The rest of the story had left her in a state of perpetual anxiety and heartbreak, searching for a daughter who might well be dead in spite of her unflinching faith that Lucy was alive.

Hawk was convinced that the answer to whatever had happened to Lucy lay somewhere in the rest of Alonsa's story. The more he knew about the intimate details of her life, the better chance he'd have of hitting on the one fact that would lead to solving the mystery of the disappearance and the phone calls.

"How did your parents feel about Todd?"

"They loved him at first. He was a charmer. People liked him instantly, especially women. He was like you in a way."

"Ouch."

"Don't worry. There's a big difference between the two of you. His charisma was all on the surface. Once you got to know him, you realized how shallow he was. Not that I admitted that to myself for a long time.

"You, on the other hand, are not only a gorgeous hunk, but you have depth and character. The better I know you, the more enticed I become."

"Kind of like Texas."

"If Texas were a sensual, exciting, heart-stopping lover."

An edgy wariness attacked his gut. She was reading way too much into last night, seeing things in him that weren't there and never would be.

"Where are your parents now?" he asked, changing the subject.

"In Anchorage. I grew up in Phoenix, but Dad got transferred to Alaska while I was in college. It was a big cultural and climate adjustment, but they both love it. Mom spent three months with me helping me cope and take care of Brandon after Lucy disappeared. She hated Texas humidity, but she was a trooper."

"What's your parents' take on the tormenting phone calls?"

"I've never told them. They'd worry too much about me and about Lucy. I try to spare them that. I've told them about you, though. Mom is praying daily for your success in finding Lucy."

"Tell her to keep that up." He needed one good, solid lead. If it came straight from heaven, fine by him.

Then she changed the subject. "It must have been fun for you growing up on a ranch in Oklahoma."

"Tons of fun." If you were into living with a drunk who mistook you for a punching bag, he silently added.

"Did you have horses and four-wheelers and ride in rodeos?"

"All of the above."

"This isn't a game where you have to answer in five words or less, Hawk."

"Sorry. Guess I've got a lot on my mind. Maybe we should go back to the subject of Texas."

She moved her hand to his neck and trailed meandering paths from his ear to his shoulder with her fingertips. "Let's just say I find more to love about Texas every day."

She was definitely reading too much into him. Still he couldn't wait to take her in his arms again.

THEY STOPPED FOR A QUICK burger in the Woodlands and it was half past two in the afternoon when they arrived at the Double M to pick up Brandon, Carne and Alonsa's car. Hawk had planned to stay behind, but Alonsa had other ideas.

She was taking this Texas thing seriously and she wanted him to take a ride around her ranch with her and discuss what she'd have to do if she wanted to start with a few head of cattle and a couple of horses.

He just wanted to be with her, even with their three-year-old chaperone around.

He pulled up right behind her in the drive. Carne bounded from the car the second she opened the back door. His barking was even more excessive than usual. He stopped at the steps to the porch and growled as if he were scaring away demons.

"Does he always carry on like that when you've been away from the house?" Hawk asked.

"No. He only does that when strangers he doesn't like are around. I don't know what's got into him today. Maybe he smells a possum or an armadillo."

"Could be." But Hawk wasn't comfortable with taking that for fact. "Why don't you get back in the car and let me take a look around before you go inside?"

Apprehension shadowed her dark eyes. He hadn't

meant to spook her, but they were in an isolated area and he'd learned the importance of caution much too well to ignore it now.

"If you think someone's in my house we should call the sheriff."

"You'd take the sheriff over a navy SEAL?"

"You don't have a weapon."

"I have a rifle in my truck. I'll take it in with me, but I could beat out a sheriff even without it." He wasn't sure that was true, but it sounded good and he figured it would ease Alonsa's mind.

"Go, SEALs." She handed him her keys, then glanced at Brandon asleep in his booster seat.

"Let him sleep. I'll come back and carry him in once I check the house. This is just a precaution. I'm not expecting trouble, but if it arises, lock the car and call Cutter."

Hawk had his doubts about immediate response to a 911 call. He had none about Cutter, and he was only minutes away. He went back for his rifle, then walked past Carne and onto the porch.

The front of the house was secure, locked and closed tight. He fit the key in the lock and opened the door cautiously, waiting and listening before stepping inside. Carne stopped barking and followed him in, his tail wagging as if they'd crossed the danger zone and all was safe again.

A few minutes inside the house and Hawk agreed with that assessment. As far as he could tell, nothing was amiss and there were no burglars or troublemakers lurking about.

He stooped and gave Carne a few solid pats. "Good

job, but next time try to let me know it's just a visit from a four-legged creature you're warning us about."

"All's clear," he announced as he approached the car. "I'll get Brandon and come back for your luggage."

"Thanks."

She grabbed her makeup bag and purse from the front seat while he unlatched the booster seat and lifted Brandon. The kid opened his eyes for a second, saw it was Hawk and let his head fall back to Hawk's shoulder.

A knot swelled inside Hawk's throat, choking him so that he could barely swallow. He wasn't sure he'd ever held a kid this size before. In fact, he couldn't remember holding a kid of any size before.

Alonsa stopped at the mailbox. He walked past her and into the house, the knot growing larger while his thoughts drifted into a dark mire of memories.

He wondered if his father had ever carried him like this. If so, how could he go from this feeling of protectiveness to the way he'd treated Hawk? How could he go so far as to—

He stiffened and felt the burn of acid in the pit of his belly. He would not go there. It was all in the past.

He pushed Brandon's bedroom door open with his foot and crossed the room, stepping over blocks and a toy tractor before reaching the bed. A picture of Brandon as a baby in Todd's arms sat on the bedside table. He studied it as he lay Brandon on the bed so that his head rested on the plump pillow.

He wondered what thoughts and feelings had flooded Todd's mind when he'd held his baby son and if he would have done things differently with Alonsa if he'd known he had so little time.

Brandon was a good kid. He'd need a dad equal to the task of loving him the way his own father never got a chance to do. Hawk was not fool enough to believe he was that man.

A low cry echoed in his ears. The kind of agonizing cry a man who'd seen men die never forgot. He heard it again, only this time he knew it wasn't just in his head.

Alonsa.

Panic and adrenaline collided inside him and he hit the stairs at a dead run.

Chapter Twelve

Alonsa was standing at the kitchen table gripping its edges so tightly her knuckles had turned white. Taut blue lines corded her neck and forehead. Hawk scanned the area quickly. There was no blood, no sign of injury or of an intruder.

It could have been another call, except that he hadn't heard the phone ring. He stepped behind Alonsa and circled her waist, pulling her close.

"What's wrong, baby?"

"This." She let go of the table and picked up a snapshot from the top of a stack of mostly unopened mail.

He took the picture from her shaking fingers. His stomach rolled, and he understood the agony he'd heard in Alonsa's cry.

The picture was of Lucy, older than she'd been in the pictures that filled Alonsa's house, but there was no doubt in his mind it was her. She was sitting in a field of flowers, smiling.

Only the flowers weren't really flowers, he noted upon closer inspection. They were splatters of blood falling from what appeared to be the mangled body of a dead baby that Lucy was cradling in her arms. A message had been scribbled across the bottom of the picture.

Help me, Mommy!

This was as sick as anything Hawk had ever seen and he'd seen a lot.

"Where did you get this?"

"It was inside that manila envelope. There was no note, just the picture. It was stuffed into the box with the regular mail."

He picked up the envelope, touching only one corner on the chance it held fingerprints. Alonsa's name was on the front in what looked like a child's printing. There was no address and no return address. No other marks of any kind.

It had to have been hand delivered. It must have been the sender's scent that Carne had picked up, suggesting the intruder had at least been on the porch. There had been no sign she or he had tried to break in to the house.

Alonsa started to shake. "It's Lucy. She must be alive. But what kind of hell is she living in?"

He placed the envelope on the table and studied the photograph. "She may not be living in any kind of hell."

"How can you look at that picture and say that? She's holding a dead baby." Her voice bordered on hysterical.

"She's smiling," Hawk said.

"That makes it worse. My Lucy. My poor Lucy. What has this monster turned her into?" Shudders shook her body and she broke into heaving sobs.

He held her, comforting her as best he could while he analyzed every aspect of the photograph. When the worst of the sobs had subsided, he let go of her long enough to grab a paper towel and wipe the smeared tears from her face.

She took it from him and blew her nose.

"It may not be nearly as bad as you think, Alonsa."

She jerked away from him. "Don't lie to me, Hawk. I'm not stupid. I know what I see."

"Then sit down and take another look."

She didn't sit and when her gaze fastened on the snapshot, tears again welled in her eyes. She held her stomach and gagged. "I think I'm going to be sick."

"How long after the abduction do you think this picture was taken?" he asked, trying to get her to reach past the horror to a semblance of objectivity.

She sniffed and grabbed another paper towel. "At least a year."

"She looks healthy," he said. "No sign of malnourishment, visible bruises or scars."

"She's holding a dead baby. What if this is part of the baby ring? What if they made her kill it or watch them do it? It's all my fault. I should have held on to her hand. I should have found her long before now." She turned away. "I can't bear it, Hawk. I just can't."

"Do you have a magnifying glass in the house?"

"In the drawer beneath the coffeepot, but I don't want to see more."

Hawk did. He retrieved the magnifier and studied the minute details. "Take a look at the baby's face."

She turned away. "You look. I've seen enough."

"I don't think that's a real baby. And even if it is, the hands holding it have been altered. They don't fit exactly right on Lucy's wrists."

"What are you getting at?"

"That may well be an older Lucy in the picture, but someone familiar with computerized photography has doctored everything else you see, right down to the flowers that look like blood."

Alonsa finally gathered the courage to take the magnifier and see for herself what he was describing.

"Hold the magnifier close, but don't touch the picture," he cautioned. "We'll get it to the FBI for a fingerprint check. They should be able to get a faster turnaround than local authorities."

"I didn't think of that. I've already touched it and the envelope."

"They may still be able to get a usable print."

"It does look altered. Even if that's a real baby, Lucy may not be holding it." Her voice was hoarse from the sobs but there was relief there, too. "Whoever took Lucy didn't kill her, Hawk. If they were going to they wouldn't have waited a year. And this may be more recent than that."

The tears spilled down her cheeks again. "Lucy's alive. I've always tried to convince myself of that, but I could never be certain. Now I am."

It sounded good, but Hawk wasn't nearly as sure of that as Alonsa. That wasn't the only concern. If Lucy was alive, she was apparently with the mentally and emotionally unbalanced person who'd orchestrated this photograph. Undoubtedly the same deranged person who'd made the phone calls.

"We have to find her, Hawk. We have to."

That he agreed with, and soon. The hand delivery of the nightmarish photo indicated not only that the person knew where Alonsa lived but that his or her mental state was likely deteriorating.

Alonsa stepped away from the table and shoved her hair back from her face. "Why? Why do this to me? How can someone want to hurt me like this?"

That was the question they had to answer before her tormentor upped the ante again and with it the danger to Alonsa.

"I've thought and thought about this," Alonsa said. "I've never done anything to deserve this and Lucy definitely hasn't. It just doesn't make sense."

She was growing agitated again. With good reason, Hawk noted.

"Do you still have that wine?" he asked.

"In the back of the refrigerator. I chilled it this weekend, but never opened it."

"I think a glass may be in order now. It will help you unwind before Brandon wakes up from his nap raring to go."

She nodded. "I'll get the glasses and the corkscrew."

They took the wine to the front porch and talked while they sipped the fruity chardonnay. There were no more tears, but Hawk knew Alonsa's nerves were shot and that she'd see that picture in her mind every time she closed her eyes until Lucy was home again.

Who could do this to Alonsa and to an innocent little girl?

He wouldn't breathe easy again until he found out. And then he hoped heaven would have mercy on the kidnapper's perverted soul, because he wouldn't have any on their life.

Until then, he'd make sure Alonsa and Brandon were never in this house alone.

HAWK KICKED AT THE SHEET and tried to find a way to get comfortable on a bed that was much too soft. He could sleep on the ground or on a hard navy bunk without any problem, but a spongy mattress made him feel as if he was drowning in a thick sea of cotton.

He'd been relegated to the downstairs guest room in Alonsa's meticulously decorated house. He wasn't about to leave her alone, and neither he nor Alonsa would have gone along with his sharing her bed whenever Brandon was around to question the arrangement.

Hawk had spent the latter part of the afternoon dealing with the situation. He was driving into Houston tomorrow afternoon to deliver the picture and the manila envelope to an FBI agent there. Craig Dalliers had promised to get in touch with them before then to request an expedited fingerprint check.

Alonsa was spending the day with Linney. When she picked up Brandon from preschool, she'd go back there and stay until Hawk returned from Houston.

The local sheriff and his deputies would be doing regular drive-bys of Alonsa's house and also watching the road in. Hawk had contacted a security surveillance company that Cutter had used before to install cameras on the gate coming onto Alonsa's spread and on the outside of her house.

And Cutter was arranging for highly dependable off-duty police protection for Alonsa when Hawk wasn't available.

As traumatic as receiving the picture was for Alonsa, it had refueled the investigation. Now Hawk just needed to get a few hours of shut-eye so *he'd* be refueled.

His mind went back to Alonsa. Days ago Cutter had

asked if he was falling for her. At this point his answer would have to be no. He'd already fallen and fallen hard.

But it changed nothing.

Finally he drifted into the twilight zone where reality blurred with the subconscious. He was back in the B&B, watching as Alonsa stepped out of a slinky black dress and stood in front of him wearing nothing but a pair of see-through lace panties that barely covered her soft triangle of dark hair.

Her body started to sway erotically and she took his hand and coaxed him to dance with her. They were both naked now, their bodies pressed together while hers made moves that were driving him out of his mind.

The music squeaked.

Immediately Hawk jerked to full wakefulness, his body tense and fully alert. The squeak sounded again. Someone was descending the staircase. He slid off the bed and stepped to the door just as Alonsa reached the bottom step.

She was wearing a ruby-red, slip-like nightie that cupped her breasts and then flared out to fall like a silky scarf somewhere above mid thigh. A short robe was thrown over her shoulders but did nothing to detract from the spell-binding view. He stood and stared, not trusting himself to speak.

"I couldn't sleep," she said. "I thought a glass of milk might help. Did I wake you?"

"No," he lied. "Milk sounds good. Want company?"

"I'd love some."

He got the glasses. She filled them and scooted one toward him before curling up in a chair catty-corner to his.

"Do you always sleep in a…"

"A negligee?" she asked, finishing his question for him.

"Yeah, one of those."

"I have a weakness for provocative lingerie. Not that I'd ever walk around Brandon dressed like this."

"Hence the robe?"

"Right, though he never gets out of bed during the night. If he wakes from a bad dream or needs something, he calls and I go to him."

"Nice to know."

"I'm glad you were up, Hawk. I don't think I ever thanked you properly for holding me together this afternoon."

"No need to. That's what I'm here for."

"Had you not been here when I opened that envelope, I don't know what I would have done."

"Had an agonizing few minutes just the way you did and then pulled yourself together."

"I'm not so sure of that. I don't seem to be able to do without you these days."

Hawk grew uneasy. He didn't like where this conversation seemed to be heading. "You just feel that way because I'm searching for Lucy. Once this is over, you won't need anyone, especially me."

"I think maybe I will. I like us together, Hawk. I like the way we fit and the way we make love."

His chest tightened and his mouth felt like he'd filled it with grit. "I like us together, too. Just don't read too much into it, Alonsa. I'm not the man you're making me into."

Her mood changed in an instant. She exhaled sharply

and crossed her legs, swinging the right one furiously. "Why do you withdraw like that every time I try to get close to you? I wasn't suggesting we move in together or start planning a wedding. I just wanted you to know that I'm crazy about you and I think we're good together."

"Then just disregard my statement."

"We made love," she said, clearly not disregarding. "Not 'had sex' but made love. I know the difference and it takes two to do that."

"I don't want to argue with you about this tonight, Alonsa. You've had enough to deal with today." He finished his milk, carried his glass to the sink and rinsed it. "We should both try to get some sleep."

Her expression softened. "Is there someone else? Did you leave someone behind when you moved here that you're still in love with?"

"My God, Alonsa. Do you really think I made love to you like that last night when I had feelings for someone else?"

"I had to ask, Hawk. I have to know."

Exasperation peppered his nerves. "There's no one else. There hasn't been for years. Now go to bed. We'll talk more tomorrow."

He walked off and left her sitting at the table. He didn't want to hurt her. He should have never let things get this far between them.

He collapsed onto the bed, wide-awake now with no dreams of Alonsa dancing though his mind. There were only the harsh truths of reality. He didn't have what it took to make her happy. He never would.

"This is about your mother, isn't it?"

He groaned and stared at Alonsa standing in his doorway with her shapely hip propped against it and her breasts peeking out from the red lace. Would this never end?

"This has nothing to do with my mother."

"Then it's your father. You always change the subject and pull into yourself when I ask about your life on the ranch."

The muscles in his stomach clenched. "Let it go, Alonsa."

"What happened between you and your father, Hawk? What happened on that Oklahoma ranch?"

He sucked in a deep breath. She wasn't going to give up and go to bed and what did it matter anyway? She probably deserved the truth after he'd come on to her when she was vulnerable and depending on him. And he'd certainly pried into her life enough.

"Okay, Alonsa. You want to know why I'd make a rotten husband and father? I'll give it to you straight."

"Not the five-words-or-less routine, Hawk. I won't settle for that."

"Twenty or more, with no interruptions from you until I'm done."

She dropped to the edge of his bed. "I'll take that."

Chapter Thirteen

"I don't remember much about my mother. She left my dad and me the year I started first grade. I got tired of people asking me when she was coming home and finally started telling them she was dead. I never heard from her. No cards or gifts or pictures, so basically she was dead to me."

"How sad. Have you ever—"

Hawk put up a hand to halt her comment.

"Right," she said. "No interruptions."

"Things didn't change much after she left except that instead of her cooking our meals, an elderly Hispanic woman came in every evening and put a meal on the table. The rest of the time I ate cereal or peanut butter sandwiches."

Alonsa bit back the sympathy, though she certainly felt enough. The only time Hawk had looked at her since starting the grim explanation was when he'd signaled her to keep quiet. He was staring straight ahead now, talking in a monotone as if the story were a recitation that didn't affect him at all.

Only it did affect him. Even now his body language

shouted that he'd withdrawn not only from her but from himself.

"My dad was a hulk of a man with a deep laugh that sounded like it came from deep in his belly. He told jokes and clapped people on the back and could spit a stream of tobacco off the porch of our little house and never get a drop of it on the banister.

"All the wranglers who worked for him liked him. They liked me, too. They taught me to ride a horse and rope a calf and, when I was older, how to cinch up an ornery bronco and ride him rodeo-style. But they were all the friends I had. I never invited anyone from school to visit. I never knew when Dad would hit the whiskey and I was afraid of what he might do to them."

Hawk stood and started to pace the small guest room. His muscles were flexed, his abs ripped, his biceps defined and rock-hard. He was every inch a man, yet she could see the frightened little boy in him and it touched her in a way his hero status never could.

"I guess I loved him in a way," Hawk said. "It never occurred to me not to. He was my dad. But when he got drunk, he got mean. I tried to stay out of his way, spent lots of nights sleeping outside on the ground or sneaking in the bunkhouse and climbing in an empty bunk.

"Sometimes there was no staying out of his way. Those were the nights he beat me."

Hawk stopped pacing and stared out the window, moving the dainty white lace curtains back with his rough hand. She ached to go to him, lay her face against his broad shoulders and wrap her arms around his waist.

He was so deep inside himself now, so cut off from her and the man he'd become that he might not even feel her body pressed against his. But if he did, he'd stop talking and he needed to get this out as much for him as for her.

"Oddly the most vivid memories for me are the first time he beat me and the last. The others all run together. The first time was right after my mother left. I was crying for her and he yelled at me to shut up. When I didn't, he kept yelling and cursing, telling me I was the reason she'd left and that I was the sniveling kid they'd never wanted in the first place."

And he'd been only six. The age Lucy was now. What if someone were doing these things to her Lucy?

Alonsa internalized Hawk's hurt, pulling it into her heart and meshing it with her own until her chest felt like it was etched with barbwire. How could anyone do that to a child?

But people did. Hawk was living proof of it.

Hawk propped his hand on the window frame. "Sometimes his belt buckle would cut me up so bad that the open wounds hurt too much the next day for me to wear clothes. I'd stay inside and watch TV and tell myself it was worth the beating because I was missing school.

"It was like a holiday in some ways because Dad was always sorry after he'd beat me. He wouldn't say it, but he'd be really nice for a few days. Super Dad, I'd call him. He liked that."

He stayed quiet so long she thought he was through talking, but still he didn't leave the window and never once turned to make eye contact.

"What happened the last time?" she finally whispered. "What made it finally stop?"

"A gun."

His voice dropped so low she had to strain to hear him. She eased to the foot of the bed so she'd be closer.

"The older I got the worse the beatings got. The week after my sixteenth birthday I came home about six on a Saturday night after winning my first bronc-riding competition. I was flying high and couldn't wait to tell Dad about winning."

Hawk's shoulders sagged now as if he were folding in on himself.

"He was drunk. And I was as strong as he was by then and in no mood for it. When he hit me, I punched him back. He went to the kitchen and got a fish knife. The first slash cut deep and I didn't have a chance after that. He cut me up bad. I thought he might have killed me."

"What happened then?"

"He passed out and I crawled outside and did the same, only I was unconscious because I'd lost so much blood. One of the wranglers found me in the morning lying in a pool of my own blood. He took me to the owner's house and they got me to the hospital. I never told anyone who'd left me in that shape and the owner and the wranglers never asked."

Because they knew. They had to know that Hawk was getting beaten all those years, but no one ever stopped it. The sin of it was on all their heads, but no one had paid like Hawk.

"I'd made up my mind while I was in the hospital that I was leaving the ranch. I figured I could find a job wrangling for another rancher in the area. I'd been doing it since I was six. I liked doing it."

"Did you leave?" she whispered.

"No." Finally Hawk turned and faced her. "When I got home I found my dad's body and a note. He'd put a pistol inside his mouth and pulled the trigger. The note just said he loved me and that he was sorry. He'd never once said those words to me while he was alive."

She pulled her feet onto the bed and hugged her legs to her chest the way she longed to hug Hawk. It was easy to see how he'd become such a hero in the service. He'd been proving himself over and over. He still was. Only now he was the one beating himself up.

"You're not that little boy any longer, Hawk."

"I know that. It's over and done, but I am who I am, Alonsa. I shut off my emotions years ago and there's no spigot for turning them back on."

"The spigot's not turned off, Hawk. You purposely withdraw. You close yourself off and try not to feel, but you still have emotions."

"Don't lecture, Alonsa. I've had enough of those in my lifetime."

"I'm just trying to reach you, Hawk."

"Don't. I told you what you wanted to hear. Now just let it go."

"What exactly does that mean, Hawk? That I shouldn't care about you, that I shouldn't want you in my life? That we shouldn't kiss or touch or make love because you might inadvertently feel something and blow all your excuses for not forming attachments?"

"We can play it any way you want, Alonsa. When this is settled and you're safe and we know exactly what's become of Lucy, I can either stay or go. Just don't go building your life around me. I'll only let you down."

He had it all down pat. Love them and leave them so ending up alone would never be his fault. She wasn't a psychologist, but she could see through that theory.

"I'm sorry for what happened to you growing up, Hawk, but it's time you stop selling yourself short. You connect just fine when you choose to connect.

"You connect with your SEAL buddies. You connected with me for a while today, being there for me when I was hanging on to stability by a thread. You've even connected on some level with Lucy and you've never even met her."

She stood and walked to the door, fighting to hold back her tears. She wanted to fall into Hawk's arms, but not when the end result would be him pushing her away.

"If you let me down it will be because you're afraid of losing again the way you lost your mother and father. Well, I'm scared of losing, too, Hawk. I'm scared of losing a chance to find out what we could be together. I'm scared of never finding out if we could make each other happy for the rest of our lives.

"All I want is a chance. You decide if you're willing to give that to us."

Tears burned her eyes when she walked away. Immediately after Hawk had dealt with his childhood demons was probably not the best time to have issued an ultimatum. But she'd had a horribly rotten day, too.

She was emotional. And she'd meant every word that she'd said. She'd love a chance with Hawk but she couldn't make that happen by herself.

She went upstairs, but instead of going to her room, she went to Lucy's. She threw herself across the flowered quilt and wet it with her tears. In spite of anything Hawk might think about himself, he was a man you could depend on. He'd find her precious daughter and bring her home.

If Alonsa never received another blessing, having Lucy home again would be more than enough to make her grateful for the rest of her life.

HAWK FOUGHT THE NOONTIME traffic with the ferocity he'd once reserved for incoming fire. Better to focus on the idiot drivers weaving from one lane to another at seventy miles an hour than to think about Alonsa.

He'd given her what she wanted, dug up memories he'd devoted half his life to forgetting, but was she satisfied? No way. She still had some half-cocked notion that they could make a go of a relationship if he'd just give it a chance.

She thought he was scared instead of scarred.

Scared. Him. Hawk Taylor, navy SEAL. Well, baby, he wasn't scared of anything.

Except of not making love to Alonsa again.

He might as well face the fact. He'd wanted her so badly this morning he was almost reduced to begging her to drive into town with him so they could make a return visit to the B and B.

But making love to her wouldn't solve the problem. It would only complicate the issues and make him want her more.

He changed lanes so he could take the Hardy Toll Road exit. It would get him to town quicker and avoid some of the traffic. He was eager to get the picture and the envelope it had come in to the FBI agent Craig had contacted.

One good definitive fingerprint could lead them to Lucy's abductor. He was a lot more worried about that little girl than he'd admitted to Alonsa. When you were dealing with a psychopath anything could happen.

His cell phone rang. He flipped on the speaker switch so he could keep his eyes on the road and his hands on the wheel.

"Hawk Taylor."

"Morning. It's Mitch Gavin, Todd's friend."

"Yeah. What's up?"

"I've been looking at that picture and trying to figure out where I might have seen that woman before."

"Any luck?"

"I'm not sure but I think it could be that stalker babe I told you about."

"Michele."

"Right, or something similar to that. She looks different in the drawing than she did in the picture I saw, but I swear there's something about it that makes me think of her—maybe the eyes. She might just be crazy enough to pull a stunt like that."

"I'll need more than Michele. Is there any way you can get me a last name?"

"You can call Craig Dalliers. He'll know it. He's the one who fired her."

"Whoa, buddy. Are you saying that Michele worked for the FBI?"

"She was one of their best agents before she went bonkers and started making up lies and sabotaging Todd's cases. I told you that, didn't I?"

"You said she got fired. You never said she worked with Todd. But, hey, it's cool. I'm just glad you called."

More than glad. He wasn't going to break his arm patting himself on the back yet, but he might have just hit the jackpot.

He called Craig the second he broke off with Mitch, but got his voice mail. He left a message for Craig to call him ASAP. Too bad they hadn't sent Craig a copy of the sketch. He might have come up with an ID last week.

It had never crossed his mind that the FBI could have searched for Lucy's abductor for two years and just plain overlooked a suspect who'd sprung right out of their midst. It was like never expecting the serial killer to live next door.

But maybe not. If she'd required cosmetic surgery after the car crash she might look significantly different than when she worked for the Bureau.

Since Michele had worked for the Bureau, her prints would definitely be on file. If she was guilty, one good print on either the picture or the envelope could seal the deal against her.

Then all that would be left was to track her down and hope for the miracle that Lucy was still alive.

He started to call Alonsa, but decided to wait until he'd talked to Craig. She'd had her hopes crushed too many times already.

But this time he had a gut feeling that they were on a roll.

"YOU'RE PREGNANT? Really?"

Alonsa jumped from the porch step where she'd been sitting and pulled Linney into a hug. "This is so exciting. How long have you known?"

"I got the official word from the doctor yesterday after you guys picked up Brandon. I had no idea. I'd just gone in for my regular checkup and he asked me about my period."

"Surely you keep up with that."

"Normally, but with the big party for Marcus and Dani and everything else that's been going on, I just didn't notice I was almost three weeks late."

"Have you told Cutter?"

"Last night. I couldn't wait. He's ecstatic."

"Well, I guess. Lucky kid to have you two lovebirds for parents."

"I'll have lots of questions to ask you about pregnancy. You know, you should move in with us until your situation blows over."

"I can't do that."

"I don't see why not," Linney insisted. "We have plenty of room and it would be safe here for you and Brandon. Cutter and Hawk are both here some of the time and Aurelio is here 24/7. Not to mention that I have three wranglers working for me now."

"I can't impose on you like that."

"You wouldn't be imposing. At least stay here days, and Hawk can stay at your place nights when he's not away working the case. And it will just be until they arrest whoever left that picture in your mailbox yesterday."

"We'll see," Alonsa said, "but after spending this morning with me and Carne and having Brandon join us after preschool, you may renege on that offer."

"Not a chance," Linney protested.

"I would like to spend some time with you, though," Alonsa admitted. "I need to pick your brain."

"About what?"

"I'm thinking of acquiring a small herd of cattle and I need information on what brands I should invest in."

Linney's brows arched. "You're going into ranching."

"You sound surprised."

"A little, but pleasantly so. You always talked of moving back to New York. I got the impression you didn't really like it in Dobbin."

"It took some getting used to, but I've given this a lot of thought and I think it's where I'd like to raise Lucy and Brandon. When Lucy comes home, she'll need lots of security and lots of time with me. I want to be able to give her both of those. I think it will be easier to make that happen here."

Linney reached over and hugged her. "You're so brave, Alonsa. I don't know if I could have the courage you do."

"You mean because I plan my life assuming that we'll find Lucy?"

"I didn't mean it to come out that way, but you do keep up such a brave front and try to stay positive."

"I'm not brave for believing Lucy will be returned to me, Linney. I'm just not strong enough to face the thought that she might not."

Nonetheless, Alonsa was determined to make plans that worked for her, with or without Hawk Taylor. Her feelings for Hawk ran deep, stronger than she'd have ever imagined she could feel for any man in so short a time.

She might even love him. But his past and the way he handled it might not ever let him love her.

"Will you excuse me for a minute, Linney? I need to call Esteban and see what he has on his schedule for me this week. If I'm going to buy cattle I'd better start earning some money."

"If Esteban needs you to make a call this afternoon, I'll be glad to watch Brandon for you."

"I can't ask you to. You're pregnant. You don't need a rambunctious kid to watch."

"That's exactly what I need. I can use the practice."

"In that case, I just may take you up on the offer."

Better to stay busy than to mope around because Hawk had practically pushed himself out of her life.

HAWK'S APPOINTMENT was for one o'clock. He'd arrived twenty minutes early and expected to have to wait. Instead the young receptionist ushered him straight into the office of FBI Agent Sylvia Colby.

Agent Colby looked to be in her early thirties, with nice legs and pretty hair. No wedding band. If he hadn't been downright dizzily infatuated with Alonsa, he might have returned her smile with a little more enthusiasm. As it was, the only action he was looking for was on his prints.

She examined the picture through the plastic bag. Her expression turned grim. "That is really sick."

"Yeah."

"And you're trying to prove the person who sent it abducted the little girl in the picture?"

"The girl's Lucy Salatoya and there's a history of the girl's mother being tormented by this woman ever since she stole her daughter."

"Lucy Salatoya. Isn't that the little girl who was taken from the Houston Zoo a few years back?"

"Two years ago. Are you familiar with the case?"

"I wasn't in Texas at the time, but I remember the situation. Her father was an agent in the New York office before he was killed in a drug bust."

So she did have some facts. His interest heightened. "Did you ever hear of a woman named Michele who worked in that same office? I don't know her last name, but she was fired for manipulating evidence."

"Are you talking about Michele Ballentine?"

"Could be. What's her story?"

"It's in the FBI annals of weird agent tales. I don't see why I can't share it with you since it made all the newspapers at the time."

"I'd love to hear it." In fact he couldn't wait.

"She was fired for tampering with evidence and then going to outlandish measures to cover up her crime. She went berserk and somehow wormed her way back into the office one night and slashed hundreds of files. Then she filed suit to get her job back saying her behavior was caused by undue stress from the firing."

"Do you have any pictures of her?"

"I'm sure we have a file on her, but it may not include photos. Charges were dropped when she checked herself into a mental hospital."

Even if they were available, the photos might not be accurate at this late date, especially after the car crash.

"What about aliases?"

"If they're known they'd be in there, too. Why?"

"I think Michele Ballentine may be the abductor whose prints we're looking to find on that very sick photo."

"Disney was right. This is a small, small world."

An hour later Hawk left the building flying high. He

had a lot more than Michele Ballentine's name, rank and serial number, or the FBI equivalent thereof. He had hospital records and a collection of aliases.

Hopefully something from his cache would lead them to Michele. Even without the fingerprints, he had a strong hunch that she was the abductor and responsible for the calls and the disgusting photo.

He couldn't wait to tell Alonsa, but maybe he should. Then he could tell her face-to-face and see her eyes light up when he broke the news that the investigation was now on solid ground.

One big worry still existed and there was no way he could prepare Alonsa for it. So he just had to hope that when they found Lucy she was still alive.

IT HAD BEEN SEVEN YEARS to the day since Todd had persuaded Michele to abort their baby. She should never have listened to him, should never have destroyed the tiny life that would have held the best of both of them. The baby would have bound him to her the way Lucy and Brandon had bound him to Alonsa. If she'd had his baby, he'd have stayed with her. They would have both left the FBI and he would still be alive.

Todd had gotten so upset with her when she'd done foolish things, but she only did them because she'd loved him so much. They both knew it was his fault that she'd been fired.

He was the one who'd manipulated the evidence. All she'd done was try to cover it up so that no one would know. She'd taken the rap for him. He should have been eternally grateful. Instead he'd dumped her for Alonsa.

But it was Michele he'd really loved. He would have

realized that and come back to her if Alonsa hadn't bewitched him with her lewd dancing and her tantalizing ways. He had come around a few times after she'd coincidentally run into him and Lucy in Central Park.

That had been after her plastic surgery to restore the damage caused by the car crash. They'd had sex. He hadn't said he loved her even then, but she knew that he did. Only by then Alonsa had him too deeply in her clutches for him to escape easily. But he would have, if he'd lived that long. They were soul mates—meant to be together.

Alonsa had given Todd the daughter that should have been theirs. That's why Michele had no choice but to abduct little Lucy. If anyone should have a part of Todd in her life, it was she.

Lucy was so much like him. Sweet and loving. And funny. Life wouldn't be worth living without her. But Alonsa would never give up trying to get her back. That's why Michele had worked so hard to set up her plan. Only…she'd have to wait to carry it out if Alonsa ran much later.

The doorbell rang. Michelle glanced at the clock. Twenty past two. Still time, but she'd have to work fast.

She walked to the door, took a deep breath and opened it.

"Alonsa, I'm so glad you could make it. I was afraid you might not show. Esteban said you were having all kinds of personal problems in your life."

"A few."

"Well, don't worry. I'm very intuitive and I have a feeling all your problems are about to be over. In fact,

I can almost guarantee it. And, I hate to ask, but would you mind pulling your car into my garage? I'm expecting the gardener any minute and he'll need to blow the dirt and grass from the drive."

Chapter Fourteen

"My car's in the shop," Keidra said, as Alonsa stepped from her car into the well-organized garage. "I'd take you through the back, except that I'd hate for my cluttered laundry room to be the first thing you see."

"That's fine. Actually I prefer using the front entry when I do the initial walk-through. It gives me a better overall feel for the client's home and lifestyle."

Keidra took a remote from her pocket and closed the garage as she led Alonsa back along the front walk and through the double mahogany doors she'd left open. Alonsa took an immediate inventory of the current décor and the features she'd have to work with. The outside had done nothing for her, but the interior held significantly more promise.

"I love the wide windows, and they're on the east side of the house so they'll let in the morning sun. The fireplace is a great asset. I can think of lots of ways to give it character. The built-in bookcases may have to go, though. They dwarf almost everything else in the room."

"I was thinking the same thing. I can't wait to hear

all your ideas, but why don't we have a cup of tea first?
That way I can tell you what I like and how much I can
afford to spend. You can take it from there."

"An excellent idea."

"We can sit in the breakfast area. It's one of the rooms
that need a drastic update. The wallpaper border is absolutely gauche. But you'll see that for yourself in a
minute."

She led Alonsa through the family room and into a
spacious kitchen with a magnificent view of Keidra's
pool area. The breakfast nook was tucked away in an
alcove just off the west corner of the room.

"You just take a seat, Alonsa, and start letting those
creative juices flow. I'll get the tea. It's herbal, orange
with just a whisper of mint."

"It sounds wonderful."

"Do you take sugar, lemon or cream?"

"Lemon."

Keidra returned almost instantly with the tea. She
scooted into the chair opposite Alonsa's.

"I see what you mean about the border," Alonsa said.
"That's easy to fix. You might want to choose a new
fabric for these chairs, as well. I'll come up with some
options for you."

She sipped her tea. There was more than a squeeze
of lemon in it and some unidentifiable herb that left her
with a metallic taste on her tongue. Keidra, however,
seemed to be enjoying hers.

Alonsa took another sip. It went down better that
time. Keidra talked a mile a minute while they finished
their tea. Alonsa tried to concentrate on what she was
saying but the afternoon sun was shining through the

window and making her so sleepy she could barely hold her eyes open.

"I'm thinking I need brighter colors all through the house. My daughter is six and she loves bright colors. Would you like to see a picture of her?"

"Shhhure."

That didn't come out right. Her tongue felt like a ladle slapping against her gums. She must be coming down with something because suddenly she was feeling dizzy and light-headed. She might have to call Esteban to come get her and drive her home.

Keidra stuck a photo in front of Alonsa's face. "This is my Lucy. Isn't she a pretty girl? She looks just like her father."

Horror seeped through the murky corners of Alonsa's brain. This was the exact same photo the kidnapper had sent her except that there was no dead baby and no blood blooming in the grass.

Keidra had the unaltered photograph. But, how could she? Only the abductor had that. Keidra wasn't the...

Oh, God. Her heart pounded as the horrific truth pushed through her mind's confusion. Keidra was the deranged woman behind the torment. She had Lucy.

Alonsa struggled to focus on what Keidra was saying.

"Todd was mine first, Alonsa. He loved me until you cast your spell over him. I was going to have his daughter. He made me kill my baby. My poor dead baby never got a chance to live.

"That's why I had to take Lucy from you. But don't worry. I could never hurt her. She's part of Todd."

This was crazy. Alonsa tried to stand, but her legs refused. It was if they'd been disconnected. Her arms were numb, as well. She'd been drugged. That was the taste she couldn't identify in the tea.

"Too bad we can't chat longer, Alonsa, but I don't have much time. The school bus will be coming soon and I don't want Lucy to find you here. As soon as we leave, I'll call a friend to come over and pick her up. She'll watch her until I return from the drive you and I are going to take to Lake Houston.

"My car is waiting in a quiet, isolated spot where no one will see us or hear the gunfire when I shoot you. Then I'll just shove your body into the lake and leave your car so that it looks like a carjacking and robbery gone bad.

"I'll never get caught. I know all the ways to keep from it. The FBI trained me well before they ruined my life."

Keidra slung Alonsa's handbag over her own shoulder and then grabbed Alonsa beneath the armpits and began to drag her dead weight away from the table and through the laundry room.

Alonsa tried desperately to escape Keidra's grasp, but the connection between her muscles and brain had totally shut down.

Rubber gloves, a roll of duct tape and a pistol had been set on top of the clothes dryer, just steps from the door that led to the garage, ready and waiting to help Keidra finish her gory deed.

Alonsa had to fight back. She couldn't die like this, not when she'd just found Lucy. She had to live for her and for Brandon.

She needed Hawk, needed his strength and his

training. Needed his bravery and confidence. He'd know what to do.

Failure is not an option.

The words hammered against her skull. She couldn't fail her children. There had to be a way to escape.

She kept pushing, desperately trying for even the slightest of responses from her limbs. But they were in the garage now. Keidra draped Alonsa over the back of her vehicle and slipped her hands into the gloves. Then she took Alonsa's keys from her handbag and unlatched the trunk, leaving no doubt as to what was coming next.

Once she was stuffed in the trunk, there would be no way for Alonsa to get out. No way to save herself. No way she'd ever see Lucy again or...

"Hawk."

His name sounded almost distinct as it slipped from her mouth.

"Your lover can't save you now, Alonsa."

Hawk had been her lover. A tender, exciting, marvelous lover, and she wanted to live to make love to him again and again. He didn't think he was the man for her, but he was the *only* man for her. She could make him see that, but first she had to survive.

Her paralyzed limbs banged against the bumper of the car as Keidra shoved her inside. In what seemed mere seconds, Alonsa's wrists and ankles were bound and strips of tape were stretched across her lips.

There was a loud clunk of metal on metal and everything went dark. Alonsa heard the hum of the car's engine and the rattling sound of the garage door as it lifted.

Failure is not an option.

Only this time it was.

HAWK HAD THE PEDAL to the metal as he took the corner near Michele Ballentine's residence in the Woodlands. If he'd called Alonsa the minute he'd left Sylvia Colby he wouldn't be in this predicament. He could have caught up with her before she played into the hands of a dangerously unbalanced woman.

Thankfully his instincts had kicked in and he'd called her when he was halfway home. When she hadn't answered, he'd phoned Linney. The second Linney mentioned Keidra's name and said that Alonsa had gone to see her on business, it all clicked for him. Keidra was one of the aliases Michele had used before.

Esteban had supplied her address and had explained that Keidra had specifically requested to work with Alonsa. There was a chance Keidra Shelton was a legitimate customer, but Hawk's gut feeling shouted she wasn't.

He turned onto Michele's street. There was no sign of the cops even though he'd called 911 from the highway and told them he was about to kill someone at Michele's address. That usually brought immediate results from law enforcement.

His luck turned and he spotted Alonsa's car emerging from a driveway midway down the block. He roared toward it, adrenaline firing through him like dynamite as he pulled into the driveway and blocked the moving car.

There was no sign of Alonsa.

Grabbing the pistol he'd been licensed to carry, he jumped from his truck, pointing the weapon at the driver's head as he raced to the car.

"Put the gun down and get off my property," she demanded.

He kept the weapon aimed at her head. "Where's Alonsa?"

That's when he saw the small black pistol in her right hand. "You're not going anywhere, Michele. Now take me to Alonsa before I pull this trigger and blow you though the friggin' wall."

"I'm FBI," she said, "and I'm ordering you to get out of my way."

"You really are bucking to make my day."

His finger tightened on the trigger. A knocking clatter yanked his attention away from Michele.

Alonsa, or maybe Lucy. Someone was alive inside the trunk. His heart started bucking inside his chest as he rushed toward the rear of the car.

Michele turned, aimed her weapon at the trunk and fired, penetrating the metal with a bullet shot at close range.

Something snapped inside Hawk, releasing a fury that hurled him into instinctive action. He shot the gun from Michele's hand in a split second and cornered her, pushing the barrel of his weapon against her right temple.

"Shoot me now, navy boy. Go ahead. It won't save Alonsa. That's Lucy kicking around in the car. Her man-stealing mother is already dead."

Hawk's chest felt as if it had been struck with a million jagged fragments of shrapnel. He'd failed Alonsa. The one person in his life who'd ever touched his soul and he'd lost her to a lunatic. Lost her without ever having given their love a chance.

His grip tightened on the pistol, his mind and soul

mired now in the fierce intensity of survival that had become second nature to him. He'd never wanted to pull a trigger more.

Sirens screamed as several police cars and one ambulance surrounded them, blocking the street and rolling onto the lawn. About time they arrived.

"Drop your weapon and move away from her," a cop called.

Hawk hesitated and then a clunking noise came from the trunk of the car, louder this time. Lucy.

"Arrest this woman on murder charges," he said, dropping his gun and moving swiftly to kick in the lock and swing open the truck.

He spotted Alonsa and his breath left his lungs in a rush of heart-stopping relief. She was huddled against a spare tire in the back right corner of the trunk, arms and ankles bound and her mouth taped shut. But her eyes were open and she was breathing.

Blood rushed to his head and his heart seemed to reconstitute itself as he bent over her and removed the tape from her mouth. Her gaze locked with his as he gathered her into his arms.

"Luce…"

"I know, baby, I know," he whispered. Only he didn't know where Lucy was or what they might find.

Alonsa tried to talk but her words were slurred, her pupils enlarged and her eyes glazed, clear signs she'd been drugged. "It's okay. I've got you, baby," he crooned as he removed the bindings and searched for bullet wounds. There were none.

"The lady's been drugged. She needs an ambulance," he called. "Hop to it."

She also needed a man who wasn't afraid to take a chance on love. It had taken almost losing her for him to realize how badly he wanted to be that man.

He leaned over and put his mouth to her ear, not even sure she'd comprehend what he was saying, but knowing he had to say it.

"I love you, Alonsa."

He wasn't sure what Alonsa mumbled in response, but it sounded like *I love you, too,* and that was great by him.

The BIG YELLOW SCHOOL BUS stopped behind the line of police cars as they were wheeling Alonsa into the ambulance. She managed to turn her head just enough to see a little girl hop off. Alonsa's heart jumped to her throat. Lucy. It was her Lucy.

Mere yards away. *Alive.* Healthy. Blood zinged through Alonsa's veins and her heart swelled until it seemed it would burst out of her chest and float to the heavens.

Lucy showed no sign of recognizing Alonsa. That was okay. They had plenty of time to get to know each other all over again. Alonsa's prayers had all been answered. Lucy was coming home to stay.

Tears of happiness welled in her eyes and started to stream down her cheeks. When she turned back to Hawk, she saw that the eyes of her big, brave, unemotional cowboy were spilling over, as well.

He squeezed her hand and pressed his lips to her forehead. "Looks like you've got your daughter back."

Thanks to a miracle wrapped in the heart and soul of her cowboy warrior. A hero all the way.

Epilogue

Two months later

"Mom, Brandon's feeding his sandwich to Carne," Lucy called from the kitchen."

"Am not."

"Are so."

Alonsa sat in the living room with Linney, loving the sound of her children's voices even when they were arguing. It still thrilled her every time she heard the word *Mom* come from her daughter's mouth.

The argument between them ended in an outburst of giggles.

Linney smiled. "They sure sound like siblings."

"They act like it, too. It took a while, but even the counselor is impressed with the progress Lucy has made in adjusting to having us as her restored family. She's sleeping well, eating like a little pig and, best of all, she's happy. She's even started remembering things from before she was abducted."

"Cutter said Hawk is amazed at how quickly she and Brandon bonded."

"They're great together, though sometimes Brandon is a bit jealous at having to share me."

"I suspect he would feel that way at times even if Lucy had been here all along."

"That's what the counselor says."

"Do you have any new information about how Michele was able to abduct Lucy without anyone seeing her?"

"Yes, because she's admitting everything and claiming innocence due to her emotional instability."

"Temporary insanity?"

"Something like that. If what she told the prosecutor is true, she'd met Lucy a few months earlier when she ran into her and Todd in Central Park. When the fight started near where we were standing, apparently Lucy became frightened and dashed away from the kids. That gave Michele the opportunity she'd been waiting on while she was spying on us."

"I still don't see how she got Lucy to go with her so quietly."

"I think it helped that she'd met her before, and Michele told her she was taking her to me. As soon as they left the grounds, she drugged her and kept her that way for days. She'd rented an isolated mountain cabin in northern Georgia and made certain not to meet anyone in the area."

"So there was method to her madness," Linney said.

"Right. Basically, she just kept Lucy in the house until she'd brainwashed her into believing I'd been killed like her father and that Michele would be her new mother."

"Lucy was barely four," Linney said. "I can see how that could happen."

"Young children are naive and easily influenced," Alonsa agreed. "Thankfully, Michele did seem to love Lucy in her own way and apparently took good care of her."

Linney hugged her arms around her chest. "Still, she has to be a very sick woman."

"That's been verified. She has a lifelong history of hospitalizations for mental and emotional problems."

"Todd really knew how to pick them, didn't he? Other than you, of course."

"I'm convinced I never really knew Todd, but he was a good father. That's what I want to concentrate on now and what I want the children to remember about him."

"You, my dear, are a saint."

"No. Just a mom. You'll find out about that yourself in a little less than six months."

"I can't wait. And Cutter is already buying toys. The latest purchase is a rocking horse."

"Every cowboy needs a horse," Alonsa said.

"Speaking of cowboys and horses, I wouldn't be surprised if you went out and found both outside your door right now."

"You know I don't have horses yet." Nonetheless the noise coming through the open window did sound like a truck stopping in front of her house.

"I bet that's Hawk," Brandon called from the kitchen.

"Yippee," Lucy yelled.

Both kids and Carne bounded past them in their rush to get out the front door. Alonsa was close behind them.

Hawk stood next to a horse trailer parked at the end

of the drive, looking every inch the exciting hunk he was. Four horses, two of them ponies, peered through the slats.

Hawk tipped his Stetson. "Howdy, ma'am. I have a delivery to make to a gorgeous rancher with two boisterous kids."

"What in the world?" She walked toward him while the kids pretty much mauled him. He hugged them right back.

"Are those horses for us?" Lucy asked, pure wonder in her high-pitched voice.

"Yeah. Are those for us?" Brandon echoed.

"As long as your mother lets them stay."

What was Hawk thinking? "I can't," she stammered. "I mean, I don't have any help yet, and I know less than nothing about taking care of animals."

"Then aren't you lucky you have me?"

"But I don't have you all the time. You have a job with Cutter."

Linney joined them and coaxed Lucy and Brandon over for a closer look at the horses. She was in on this, though Alonsa didn't see how she could have gone along with it, knowing Alonsa wasn't equipped to start raising horses yet.

"Can we take a walk?" Hawk asked.

"I have the kids."

"No, you don't," Linney said. "I have them."

This was definitely a setup. Hawk put his arm around Alonsa's shoulders and led her to the tire swing.

"You should have asked me first," she said.

He pulled her into his arms. "Just settle down. I'm about to make you an offer I hope you can't refuse."

"Then it better include some wranglers."

"Honey, you won't need but one, that is as long as you say yes."

"To the horses?"

"To marrying me."

Her head began to spin. She loved Hawk like crazy but she was treading lightly, giving him time to get used to the whole idea of commitment and taking on not only a wife but two kids.

He looked perplexed. "You will say yes, won't you?"

Marry Hawk? Sleep in his strong arms every night for the rest of her life? Love him and have him love her back?

In a New York minute, except… "Are you sure you're ready for all of this?" She waved her arm to indicate the house, land and kids.

"I love you, Alonsa, more than I ever thought it possible to love another human being, and I want it all. You. The kids. A new lifestyle."

Happiness spilled from her heart, until she heard the last of his words. She wasn't asking him to change his lifestyle. She loved him just the way he was. "What kind of lifestyle change?"

"I've been a warrior long enough. I've already told Cutter that I'd like to get back to ranching. I have enough money saved to get us started with a small herd, and we can see where it goes from there."

He kissed her then, slow and wet and totally intoxicating.

"Are you ready to take a chance on a cowboy, Alonsa?"

"Yes. Oh, Hawk. Yes! As long as the cowboy is you. I love you so very much."

But taking a chance on Hawk Taylor wasn't taking a chance at all.

It was a sure thing.

* * * * *

INTRIGUE..

1210/46a

INTRIGUE...

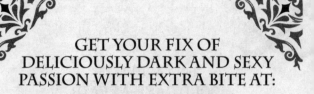

Four wicked tales of paranormal romance and supernatural seduction by bestselling authors

Divine Beginnings by **P.C. Cast**

The Amazon's Curse by **Gena Showalter**

Voodoo by **Maggie Shayne**

Edge of Craving by **Rhyannon Byrd**

Available 17th September 2010

www.mirabooks.co.uk

A Goddess of Partholon Novel

Part-human, part-centaur, Elphame has always
been different. When she's asked to breathe new
life into the remote MacCallan Castle, she's
finally found her true calling.

But Elphame hadn't banked on the bat-like
human Fomorian descendants returning to
MacCallan with their own devastating agenda.
Nor the fact that she may have finally found her
lifemate…at THE most inconvenient time!

Available 16th April 2010

www.mirabooks.co.uk

A Goddess of Partholon Novel

Born to be the Chief Shaman and ruler of a herd of centaurs would be tough for any girl – and Brighid wants out. Joining Clan MacCallan as a Huntress and helping broken-hearted Cuchulainn on his mission seems much simpler.

But Brighid realises her powers cannot lie dormant forever. And that she cannot escape her destiny.

Available 21st May 2010

www.mirabooks.co.uk

Something is wrong with Kaylee Cavanaugh…

She can sense when someone near her is about to die. And when that happens, an uncontrollable force compels her to scream bloody murder. Literally.

Kaylee just wants to enjoy having caught the attention of the hottest boy in school. But when classmates start dropping dead for no reason and only Kaylee knows who'll be next, finding a boyfriend is the least of her worries!

Book one in the Soul Screamers *series.*

Available 1st January 2011

www.mirabooks.co.uk

THE WAR HAS ONLY JUST BEGUN…

Werecat Faythe's future as Alpha is jeopardised when her father is ousted from the werecat council.

Faythe's biggest fight now lies ahead. Old allies from the supernatural world stand by her. And were-toms Marc and Jace will sacrifice themselves for her.

Yet Faythe knows that it's up to her to bring justice to her pride once and for all.

The sixth part in the Shifters *series*

Available 17th September 2010

www.mirabooks.co.uk

A DRUNK DRIVING CASE IS ONLY A DRUNK DRIVING CASE... UNTIL SOMEONE DIES

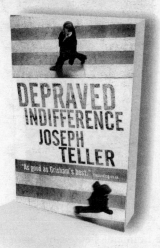

A sports car, speeding in the wrong lane, kills all nine occupants of a van – eight of them children.

Criminal defence attorney Jaywalker is serving a three-year suspension. But when a woman seduces him into representing the driver – who is also her husband – things get messy.

And when Jaywalker rounds a blind corner in the case, he collides with a truth that could change everything.

Available 16th July 2010

www.mirabooks.co.uk

2 FREE BOOKS
AND A SURPRISE GIFT

We would like to take this opportunity to thank you for reading this Mills & Boon® book by offering you the chance to take TWO more specially selected books from the Intrigue series absolutely FREE! We're also making this offer to introduce you to the benefits of the Mills & Boon® Book Club™—

- **FREE home delivery**
- **FREE gifts and competitions**
- **FREE monthly Newsletter**
- **Exclusive Mills & Boon Book Club offers**
- **Books available before they're in the shops**

Accepting these FREE books and gift places you under no obligation to buy, you may cancel at any time, even after receiving your free books. Simply complete your details below and return the entire page to the address below. You don't even need a stamp!

YES Please send me 2 free Intrigue books and a surprise gift. I understand that unless you hear from me, I will receive 5 superb new stories every month, including two 2-in-1 books priced at £5.30 each and a single book priced at £3.30, postage and packing free. I am under no obligation to purchase any books and may cancel my subscription at any time. The free books and gift will be mine to keep in any case.

Ms/Mrs/Miss/Mr _____ Initials _____

Surname _____

Address _____

_____ Postcode _____

E-mail _____

Send this whole page to: Mills & Boon Book Club, Free Book Offer, FREEPOST NAT 10298, Richmond, TW9 1BR

Offer valid in UK only and is not available to current Mills & Boon Book Club subscribers to this series. Overseas and Eire please write for details.. We reserve the right to refuse an application and applicants must be aged 18 years or over. Only one application per household. Terms and prices subject to change without notice. Offer expires 28th February 2011. As a result of this application, you may receive offers from Harlequin Mills & Boon and other carefully selected companies. If you would prefer not to share in this opportunity please write to The Data Manager, PO Box 676, Richmond, TW9 1WU.

Mills & Boon® is a registered trademark owned by Harlequin Mills & Boon Limited. The Mills & Boon® Book Club™ is being used as a trademark.